Like a hero, the sheriff rode in...

Drew McClain turned on his flashlight and threw his shoulder against the door of the abandoned shack. It creaked open and he cautiously stepped in, but before he knew what hit him, a form hurtled toward him, nearly knocking him to the ground.

"Thank goodness you came." Leslie ran to him and threw herself into his arms. "The boys called me here, but they're not here."

Before Drew could think about how good she felt against his chest, the door quietly closed behind him and there was the distinct sound of a bar locking into place from outside.

"What the heck..." A sinking feeling overtook him as his flashlight lit on a nearby table with two juice boxes, two apples and two bags of cookies—all next to a single cot.

The more he thought about it, the clearer it became. He didn't have to see Leslie's face to realize that he'd underestimated her sons' determination to get themselves a daddy. A deep laugh erupted from low in his belly.

The boys couldn't get themselves a daddy the old-fashioned way—they'd kidnapped one!

ABOUT THE AUTHOR

Mollie Molay started writing years ago when, as a going-away present, her co-workers gave her an electric typewriter. Since then, she's gone on to become president of the Los Angeles Romance Writers of America. A part-time travel agent, Mollie loves to travel, and spends whatever spare time she has volunteering; she's grateful for her good fortune and wants to give back to those around her. She lives in California.

Books by Mollie Molay

HARLEQUIN AMERICAN ROMANCE

560—FROM DRIFTER TO DADDY
597—HER TWO HUSBANDS
616—MARRIAGE BY MISTAKE
638—LIKE FATHER, LIKE SON
682—NANNY & THE BODYGUARD
703—OVERNIGHT WIFE

WANTED: DADDY

MOLLIE MOLAY

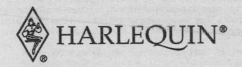

HARLEQUIN®

TORONTO • NEW YORK • LONDON
AMSTERDAM • PARIS • SYDNEY • HAMBURG
STOCKHOLM • ATHENS • TOKYO • MILAN • MADRID
PRAGUE • WARSAW • BUDAPEST • AUCKLAND

For little Michael Ross Moore—and now there are seven.
And for Debra Matteucci, who *knows* when a
story is right. Thank you.

Acknowledgment

The reader can find the reconstructed silver mining town of
Calico northeast of Los Angeles, on the highway to Las Vegas,
Nevada. While its historical background has been correctly
depicted, the actual description of Calico has been altered for
the purposes of my story. There are celebrations held
there several times a year, including the
well-known Hullabaloo Festival.

ISBN 0-373-16729-6

WANTED: DADDY

Copyright © 1998 by Mollie Molé

Prologue

"What are we going to do now, Jeremy? There aren't any men left around here willing to take on Mom."

"Well," a young voice answered after a pregnant pause, "I guess there's no help for it. We'll just have to kidnap someone we want for a dad and keep him until he agrees to ask Mom to marry him."

"Wow! That really would be somethin' awesome!"

"Yeah. 'Course, getting Mom to say yes is a whole different story. She says all of the men around here aren't worth the powder to blow them to hell."

"Us, too?"

"Nah. Heck, Tim, I'm only ten and you just turned eight. We don't count."

"So where are we going to find someone?"

"I don't know, but now that Calico Days is going on there's bound to be someone new in town who's willing to do it."

Leslie Chambers had paused beside the screen door to her weathered antique-quilt store just in time to overhear her sons' conversation. She sucked in her breath, too angry to open the door and haul in the boys and give them a piece of her mind.

Kidnap a man and force him to ask her to marry him?

She counted to ten, slowly and evenly.

Chapter One

He came from Temptation, a small town no larger than a village, deep in the farmlands of western Pennsylvania. The ironic part of it, as far as he'd been able to tell during the first seventeen years he'd resided there, was that there hadn't been a damned thing tempting about the place.

To a boy yearning to become a man, temptation had been just out of reach somewhere down the highway, across the rolling green fields and over the next hill.

As far as he was concerned, naming the town Temptation had been a cruel joke. As soon as he'd gotten his act together, he said goodbye to the aunt and uncle who'd done their best to raise him properly, and set out to find the real thing.

He'd been in and out of trouble more times since then than he could count. Temptation kept rearing its head, but had never yielded anything remotely more satisfying than the vague need for something or someone special that had begun to gnaw at him lately. He'd begun to feel as though he was looking for the elusive pot of gold at the end of a rainbow. And, just like the rainbow, whatever it was that would have satisfied his soul had always remained just beyond his grasp.

He hadn't realized how tired he was of the process of searching for a half-formed dream until he saw the slender redhead coming toward him at a fast clip down the main street of Calico, California.

Even though he had yet to be formally introduced, he recognized the newly elected lady mayor of Calico. Elected by default, that is, since no one else around town relished taking on the responsibility. The lady had a fierce temper, and was said to have ice flowing in her veins when it came to men.

Her auburn hair glistened in the hot noonday sun, and her high cheekbones were flushed. Like the rest of the residents, in keeping with the historical locale, she was wearing vintage clothing. As she came closer, he was intrigued to see hazel eyes, cat's eyes, flashing with anger. As the wind she stirred up in passing whipped around her, the fitted bodice and full skirt of her blue-and-white dimity outfit managed to reveal more of her female figure than they concealed.

He swept her with a quick glance and caught a glimpse of dust-spattered boots and close-fitting jeans showing under her dress. She was a striking combination of yesterday's and today's worlds.

Thoughtfully, he paused to enjoy the view.

She looked up and caught him studying her. For a moment she hesitated, then moved toward him with grim determination in her body language that boded no good. If she'd been a man, in another time and place, he would have had his gun out by now.

"I need your help," she announced, without the

usual preliminaries, when she skidded to a stop in front of him.

"An introduction would be a good place to start," Drew replied dryly, pushing his Stetson away from his forehead. Squinting in the sun, he took in the flash of annoyance that crossed her steady gaze. Something about that cool look irritated him and prompted him to bait her just to see what she would say next.

"You see, it's like this," he added, in what he thought was a reasonable tone of voice, "I like to know the name of people I'm asked to do business with."

Reasonable request or not, from the expression on her face, he wasn't sure she was buying.

As far as he was concerned, the next move was up to her.

Leslie Chambers took a deep breath. If she hadn't needed this man so badly, she would have told him to go straight to hell. Along with every other male who loitered along the wooden sidewalk of the reconstructed silver-mining town of Calico, California. With this man, she would have to slow down. At least long enough to be polite and introduce herself. She had no choice, unless she wanted to wait until the next likely man showed up. Fat chance. She didn't have the time. At the rate they were going, her boys would surely kill someone or themselves any time now.

"Sorry, I guess I was in a hurry," she answered. "I'm Leslie Chambers. I run the antique-quilt shop down the street." She wiped her hand on her skirt and offered it to the dark, handsome stranger.

"Drew McClain," he replied gravely as he took her hand, "but of course you already knew that, or you wouldn't have come looking for me. You *were* looking for me, weren't you?''

She frowned as she looked him over from the top of his cinnamon-colored hair to his dust-covered boots, and flushed when she saw the smile that came over his face as she checked him out. She fought the reaction stirring within her at the sight of his tall, lithe body and the lazy stance that belied the air of authority that clung to him. The knowing smile hovering around his lips told her he knew the effect he was having on her as well as she did. Under any other circumstances, she would have turned on her heel and left him standing there gaping his fool head off. Still, he'd been highly recommended by the sheriff and was obviously able to help her. About the ready and willing parts, after she told him what she wanted him for, she had her doubts.

This was no time to skirt the facts—she was prepared to call a spade a spade and take it from there. She took a dcep breath and plunged right in. ''I understand you're acting as the sheriff's deputy around here for Calico Days.''

''For a while,'' he answered slowly, his gaze challenging her, asking why.

''Good enough,'' she answered, avoiding his unspoken question. She'd tell him the whole story in her own good time. She forced a smile. ''I'd like to hire some of your spare time until the festival is over.''

When he regarded her in silence, she hurried on. ''I'm not the kind to mince words, Mr. McClain. I don't care how long you intend to hang around here as long as you stay the full week of Calico's anniversary.''

"A week?" he asked, taking a toothpick from his vest pocket. "I don't know about that. To be honest with you, I'm pretty busy with my regular job. Why do you need a week?"

"I'm not going to beat around the bush either, Mr. McClain, but I'd just as soon give you my proposition somewhere a little more private than this." She indicated the knot of men standing outside the saloon across the street regarding them with interest. "How about a cup of coffee in the café down the street?"

"It's your call, Ms. Chambers," he replied, pulling his hat over his forehead to shade his eyes. "Coffee will be fine." His expression, as he glanced over at the saloon, told her he'd much rather have met with her there, where he could have something stronger to drink than coffee.

She could feel the avid eyes of the men loitering by the saloon door boring into her back as she led the way to the Last Chance. The restaurant's name would have been better suited to a saloon, but the red-and-white calico curtains and a handwritten menu in the window gave away its true identity.

"Now, what can I do for you?" Drew asked when they'd been served by a curious waiter who hovered longer than he should have. Drew expertly dropped three lumps of sugar into the hearty pungent brew, paused and tossed in one more. "I like my drinks sweet and hot—the way I like everything else," he said suggestively into her blush, knowing full well he was being outrageous. He couldn't help himself. Something inside him wanted to separate the woman from the mayor.

"If you're trying to frighten me off," she answered with a scowl, "you have another think coming. This is a business proposition and I'll thank you to remember that!"

He shrugged. "Go ahead, I'm listening."

"I need a baby-sitter," she answered brusquely. "For my two children. Boys," she added succinctly, as if the children's gender explained her request.

Drew choked on his scalding coffee. Searing rivulets ran down his chin and onto the silver deputy sheriff's badge on his chest. A shudder ran through him. "A baby-sitter?" he asked incredulously. "Hey, lady, you've gotten your signals mixed up. You're talking to the wrong person. If you need someone to take care of a couple of kids, I'd say you're going about it in the wrong way. You need a woman for that kind of a job, don't you?"

"No, sir," she answered firmly. "I need a lawman. Someone to put the fear of God into those two boys of mine. After all I've been through, nothing less will do."

Wincing as he mopped hot coffee off his chest, Drew managed to grin through his pain. Whatever her boys had been up to, they were probably no worse than he'd been as a kid. He'd been repeatedly warned to keep his nose clean, make sure his thoughts were pure and to stay out of trouble. The first admonition hadn't been all that hard to follow. The second became more difficult as he grew older. As far as the third one went, if trouble hadn't already found him, he'd always made sure he found it.

Now, far as he was concerned, something told him

trouble was staring him in the face. And now that he'd met Leslie Chambers's angry, but breathtakingly beautiful green eyes, so was temptation. He'd never run from trouble before, he figured as he studied the spitfire seated across from him, and he wasn't about to start now. But baby-sitting was something else. However, it wasn't only curiosity that drew him to listen to her, it was the way her eyes lit up when she was angry. In fact, the angrier she became, the prettier she looked.

One thing was certain, her two boys weren't ordinary kids. Not with a mother like her.

"Why don't you start at the beginning?" he asked politely. He'd give her five minutes of his time and then he'd excuse himself. The last thing he needed was to give her any encouragement.

He signaled the hovering waiter to refill his half-empty coffee cup and muttered for him to keep it full. Whatever the lady had on her mind, he had a feeling he was going to need a lot of black, strong, hot coffee to keep his mind clear. The stronger the better. Especially since he heard trouble knocking at his door louder than ever before.

Leslie took a deep breath, glanced up at the ceiling while she gathered her thoughts and prepared to launch into a partial laundry list of her sons' latest escapades. If the man knew the whole story, he'd probably run as if the devil were chasing him.

"I won't bother you with all the details, but these last two weeks since school let out have been the last straw!"

Drew dropped more sugar cubes into his coffee, stirred slowly and raised his eyebrows. From her grim expression, one thing was clear. Whatever the kids had done sure must have been over the top to warrant the services of the law.

"How old did you say the boys are?"

"I didn't, but Jeremy is ten and Tim is eight."

Drew relaxed. Judging from their mother's agitated appearance, the kids must be a handful. Still, they were younger than he'd thought and couldn't have been *that* hard to tackle. At those tender years, they'd probably done nothing more than take two cents' worth of candy from the emporium across the street. Hardly enough reason for a lawman to take the time to investigate. He let her continue without further comment. She was clearly a woman with a story to tell.

"Go on," he encouraged. He had nothing better to do for the next few minutes—he might as well let her get whatever was troubling her off her chest.

"I'll tell you up front, the boys are incorrigible," she went on. "You won't believe what they've been up to!"

"Try me," Drew replied. He drained his coffee cup and sat back to listen.

"For one thing, they've been collecting rattlesnake skins for souvenirs to sell to the tourists."

"Not off live rattlers, I hope," he said, hiding a smile.

"No," she answered shortly, "but I wouldn't put it past them. They try to make pets out of anything that moves. The desert can be a very dangerous place to play. There are live rattlers out there, and heavens knows what else!"

Drew nodded his agreement. He didn't like rattlesnakes any better than she did. Still, the kids sounded more like a couple of entrepreneurs rather than desperadoes.

"Last week, they took my car and drove it out into the desert and into a ditch. We had to have it towed out and back home."

The look on her face dared him to make light of that escapade.

"So far, none of it sounds like a hanging offense," Drew said after a moment's thought. He smiled ruefully when he remembered taking off the garage door the first, and the last, time he'd "borrowed" his uncle's car. Retribution had been swift. He hadn't been able to sit down for two days.

Her voice took on a harder edge. He could tell her patience was wearing thin.

"If that wasn't enough, they 'borrowed' a neighbor's calf and took turns pretending they were riding a bull. Said they were practicing for the rodeo we're having at the end of the week." She paused as if to let the gravity of the situation sink in.

"Sounds about right for two kids that age," Drew said into her frown. "You're just lucky it wasn't the real thing."

"That's not all," she added, waving a hand for emphasis. "They not only let the cows out of their pasture, the cows trampled through town and scared the living daylights out of everyone!"

"Was anyone hurt?"

"Not really—a stubbed toe and a few scratches when people scrambled out of their way." She paused to take a deep breath. "Oh, and a couple of broken windows. I not only had to pay to have the windows replaced, I had to listen to dozens of complaints.''

Drew choked off laughter. ''Guess I can understand that one, too. All boys dream of joining a circus or competing in a rodeo. I've ridden in one or two myself.''

''That's no excuse!'' She glared at him for a long moment. ''I'm not through yet. Just yesterday, they took the old hearse out of the museum!''

At that, Drew straightened up. Stealing a hearse was no joke. ''Any bodies inside?''

''No! That's not the point,'' she answered, clearly frustrated.

''What would the boys want with an antique hearse?''

''They were having a funeral for one of their pets— a rabbit!''

He could hardly contain his laughter at the look of outrage that came over her face.

''Doesn't any of this tell you how much Jeremy and Tim need a man's guidance?'' she demanded. ''A sensible man, with enough authority to make it stick?'' she added meaningfully.

Her look told him louder than words that she didn't consider him any more grown-up than her boys. For the first time, he felt ashamed of teasing her. After all, she was a mother obviously concerned about her wayward kids. He was about to offer to talk to the boys when her next words registered.

''Now, they're plotting to kidnap some man!''

''Kidnap?'' He straightened up and shoved away his coffee. This one was a little more serious. ''That's a horse of another color and against the law. Who's rich enough around here to be held for ransom?''

"I didn't mention 'ransom.'" Her complexion turned even rosier than before.

"Well, then," Drew commented. "So far you haven't mentioned anything illegal. You don't need me."

"If this continues, this kidnapping thing might well turn into something illegal," Leslie said tightly. Her knuckles turned white as she clenched her hands.

"Sorry," Drew barely repressed a laugh. "It's just that everything you've told me, and the idea of two little kids plotting to kidnap a man, has to be about the funniest story I've ever heard."

"Actually," she said coldly as she rose to her feet, "after what Sheriff Carrey said about you, I expected more than facetious comments. I should have known better." Her look was enough to freeze a lesser man.

Drew sobered abruptly and eyed her thoughtfully as he remembered her reputation. The combination of concerned mother, fiery redhead and ice lady rolled up into one pert package offered contradictions worthy of consideration. From the little he'd heard about the lady mayor, there wasn't a male in town she had any use for. Finding out just what it was that had turned her against men might be interesting. Except that the effort would probably take time, and he didn't have any to spare.

His feet were itching to move on, and the last thing he needed right now was to tangle with trouble in the form of two adventuresome kids. Not now, not at this stage of his life, and not with someone whose attraction was unaccountably growing by the minute. And definitely not with someone who had two young children who needed a father to keep them in line.

"Sorry, Ms. Chambers. I might as well tell you right off. First, I already have a job. And, secondly, I don't do kids."

Her eyes narrowed. "Are you sure you won't reconsider?"

"No, ma'am. When the county sheriff, who incidentally is a friend of mine, asked me to do him a favor and take on the job of deputy sheriff for the duration of the festival, I agreed. The job might be for show, but I tend to take my responsibilities seriously."

"And so do I," she answered, as if daring him to challenge her. She studied him for a long moment— long enough for the hair on the nape of his neck to start to prickle. He had a feeling that he wasn't going to like whatever she was about to say any more than he had the rest of their conversation.

"You do understand that as mayor of Calico, I can have the sheriff order you to watch the boys?"

Drew pushed away his coffee cup, motioned away the wide-eyed waiter and rose to his feet at her blatant threat. Any attraction he'd begun to feel for her evaporated. His eyes locked with hers. He'd been patient long enough. It was time to put an end to the whole ridiculous episode. He was no baby-sitter.

"I should tell you, Ms. Chambers, that the last time I was ordered to do something I didn't want to do, I put two thousand miles between the man and myself in the space of twenty-four hours."

"Is that a threat, Mr. McClain?"

"No, ma'am." He threw a five-dollar bill on the

table, leaned over and spoke squarely into her flashing eyes. "It's a promise."

SEETHING WITH FRUSTRATION, but reluctantly admiring his declaration of independence, Leslie watched the deputy saunter out through the door. She was used to men walking out on her.

There had been no doubt in her mind Drew McClain was the type of man she needed to keep Jeremy and Tim out of trouble. But whether he was *the* man she needed for the job was another question.

The unnatural silence surrounding her in the café abruptly registered. She straightened and glanced around her. The waiter, hand poised to pick up the bill the deputy had left, dropped his arm and flushed when he caught her cool gaze. The few local residents and the dozen or so tourists, their food untouched, stared avidly at her as if waiting to see what her reaction would be to having the deputy sheriff talk to her the way he had before he left. The short-order cook and owner, Maddie Hanks, had come out from behind the counter and stood gaping.

Frank Holliday, proprietor of Calico's barbershop, evaded her eyes and turned back to his lunch. But not before he made a laughing comment to Herb Strawberry, the editor of the small newspaper that printed local news and produced souvenir newspaper front pages for tourists.

Leslie's heart sank. Of all the people who could have been in the Last Chance at that moment, why did it have to be Herb? A man whose offers to take her square dancing at the town's meeting hall she'd turned down several times and again just the other day.

And then there was Frank Holliday. She'd told him off just that morning when he'd tried to tell her how to run Calico. If he knew so much, she'd asked him, why hadn't he run for the office of mayor himself when the town had decided it needed a mayor and a town council to manage its growing prosperity? He hadn't taken her comment lightly. From the smirk on his face as he sat gazing at her, she could tell he was no friend of hers, either.

There was no doubt in her mind that one and all had heard Drew McClain turn down her request to keep her boys in line. And that everyone else in town would get an earful before the day was over. Well, she vowed, she wouldn't give them the satisfaction of running away. She signaled the waiter for another cup of coffee.

If only she could learn to keep her temper. In the last hour she'd drawn enough of the wrong kind of attention to last a lifetime. But one thing was clear. If she didn't do something about those boys of hers, she'd go broke paying off the damages they caused and become the laughingstock of Calico into the bargain. If the boys didn't manage to injure themselves first.

She hid an inward shudder as she imagined the gossip over at the barbershop. Not to mention tomorrow's newspaper headline: "Local Mayor Meets Her Match." And it took only a short mental stretch to visualize that headline calling her "Ice Lady" instead of "Mayor."

Contrary to popular belief, Leslie knew full well what the local men called her. She chose to ignore the label, to hide the hurt inside, but she cared more than she was willing to admit—even to herself.

She drained the last of her coffee, gathered the cloth purse that matched her period outfit and made for the door. As she exited, she could hear excited conversation start up behind her.

"LOOKS LIKE the ice lady's met her match!" Herb Strawberry announced with a sneer. He wiped his chin and threw down his napkin. "About time, I'd say."

"Yeah, looks that way," Frank Holliday agreed. "I'd be willing to bet the sheriff will thaw her out before the week's over!"

"Bets?"

"Yeah. We may not have gotten very far with the lady mayor, me included," Frank said ruefully, "but I'll bet the price of a shave and a haircut the new deputy will have her eating out of his hand in no time."

"Shave and a haircut?" Herb gazed thoughtfully at the door Leslie had disappeared through. "Hell, I'm willing to up the ante for a sure thing. Seems to me she's met her match. I'm betting twenty dollars on the deputy."

"Me, too," Frank answered with a broad grin on his face. "This ought to liven things up around here. Let's go over to the saloon and get a pool started."

"Good idea. Say, maybe we ought to stop at the jailhouse and let McClain in on the betting."

"Hell, no," Herb answered. "For all we know, he's the last honest man around here. We don't need to tell him anything. Besides, he said he doesn't intend to bother with Leslie or her kids."

"He doesn't want anything to do with the *kids*—not her. Though Lord knows they could use a man's strong hand." Frank shrugged. "I'm kinda glad it isn't going to be me, at that. Besides, betting that a guy like McClain can tame Leslie isn't exactly being dishonest."

"Guess you're right. And it'll be more interesting to see who's going to win if neither of them knows about the bet. That way, no one can accuse us of rigging the outcome. And, if McClain decides he has a stake in the bet," Herb added with a sly grin, "we can cut him in on the winnings later."

Chapter Two

The explosion rocked the jailhouse. The mirror hanging on the wall in front of him dropped into the sink and shattered into dozens of pieces. Windows rattled. The floor shook under his feet. Drew hit the deck. Then, silence.

"What the hell!" He grabbed his gun and holster, headed for the door and ran out into the street. Half-dressed tourists were pouring out of the small hotel next door to the jail.

Lean and spry, Maddie Hanks, frying pan at the ready, outstripped a small group of diners racing out of the Last Chance Café. Frank Holliday, in the process of opening his barbershop, stood gaping at the frenzied group heading toward him. The postmaster, Elias Broome, stood with his hand frozen to the handle of the door to the ancient post office building.

As he rushed up the street to where the blast had taken place, Drew took some comfort from the fact that it was still too early for most of the small businesses in town to have opened. By the grace of God, most of the citizens of Calico were still asleep in their beds. But they'd sure had a rude wake-up call.

With the rest of the curious pack at his heels, Drew sprinted toward the black and gray cloud of smoke that billowed into the early morning sky. The sound of the explosion still echoed against the patchwork hills. A cloud of dust hung in the air.

"For crying out loud!" Maddie huffed as she hurried along beside Drew. "Must be some fool tourist mining for silver!"

"No," he answered shortly, his eyes combing the end of the street for any sign of victims or survivors. "Anyone using dynamite around here would have had to file a permit. There hasn't been any that I know of."

"Never stopped a jackass or two...from trying to work dry mines...before now," Maddie retorted between labored breaths. "Doc Parsons has his hands full every year. People trying to get rich by mining for silver. Guess Sheriff Carrey deputized you...to keep it from happening again this summer."

"Looks like he may have been wrong, doesn't it?"

Drew could see that the smoke was coming from behind one of the buildings, and he hoped that the explosion was no more than some wild animal setting off an abandoned stick of dynamite when it had tried to eat it and, unhappy with the taste, tossed it away. And he prayed that no human being had been hurt in the mishap.

The firehouse bell sounded. Good, Drew thought as he noticed the activity at the fire station—one of the few buildings that remained ancient on the outside but was outfitted with the latest equipment on the inside. The volunteer firemen had made it to the station in record time. If there *was* a fire, at least the men would be there to handle it.

As the smoke cleared, it became even more clear that his prayers would go partially unanswered. Trouble materialized—in the form of Leslie and two young boys.

Leslie Chambers, grasping a protesting boy in each hand, appeared from behind the Quilt Lady shop. Her anger was reflected in her body language and hung around her like a dark cloak.

The older boy, Jeremy, his face and hair smudged with powder and his shirt hanging out of his pants, seemed to be putting up a strong defense. The younger, Tim, equally dirty and with jeans ripped at one knee, howled with every step.

Drew instinctively felt he knew what this was all about. Ignoring Maddie's excited exclamations, he cursed under his breath. Sure as hell his luck had run out and his worst nightmare was about to come true. He was about to be saddled with two kids. If for no other reason than to keep them alive and Calico from being blown to smithereens.

With the crowd close on his heels, Drew ground to a stop in front of Leslie. Before he had a chance to speak, she laid into him. "Well, Mr. Deputy, would you say that *this* escapade is worthy of your attention?" She glared down at the boys and back at Drew. "If it doesn't, then I would say you're no lawman!" She shook the boys into silence when they started to protest. "It's only a miracle they're in one piece. My back porch isn't!"

Reminding herself that men didn't like to be pushed,

Leslie hid her anguish at the near miss that could have taken her children. She focused on Drew, and her angry tirade sputtered out. For the first time she noticed he was half naked.

At the sight of the deputy's nude torso, her thoughts flew into the morning breeze.

The rising sun glistened on Drew's damp, cinnamon-colored hair. His face was covered with patches of shaving cream. He'd obviously just showered and had been in the process of shaving. Droplets of water nestled in the patch of dark hair on his muscular chest and were slowly making their way down to his unbuttoned waist band. His shoulders and arms, barely covered by an inadequate towel, were broad, muscular and tanned to a golden hue. His lithe torso narrowed to a slender waist.

Without a doubt, he was the sexiest man she'd ever seen.

A tingling sensation was definitely building in her middle. And at the least appropriate time and place.

Afraid that her instinctive reaction was obvious, she hastily raised her gaze from his chest to his hazel eyes. She blinked at the growing acknowledgement of her reaction she saw building there.

It was only then Drew realized he'd run out of the jailhouse partially clothed. A mental check of what he must look like reminded him his chest was uncovered, his feet bare. His belt was still undone and his jeans hung loosely on his hips. Both threatened to go south with every labored breath he took.

The look on Leslie's face sent an answering flush through him. The awareness of her response to his near-nakedness left him with mixed emotions. The last thing he needed was another complication on a day that already had enough complications to choke a horse.

With an effort, he pulled himself together. Muttering a brief apology for his appearance, he buttoned his jeans, pulled up his zipper and buckled his belt. The damp towel that hung on his shoulders didn't cover much more of him, but at least it was something.

He'd never felt more naked in his life.

And never more embarrassed.

To make matters worse, a cut he'd made on his face when the blast had occurred began to smart. He could feel a trickle of blood start to run down his cheek and onto his chin.

Leslie had fallen silent as she took in the deputy sheriff's appearance. She had never seen a man as strikingly handsome as this one before. And, under the present circumstances, she could have done without the revelation. She had a job to do and she didn't need any distractions. At least, not of the male kind. And not in the form of the man she was about to ask to do something that only a few days ago he had clearly announced he wasn't interested in doing.

His expression, as he regarded her and her boys with disgust, spoke louder than words. It was obvious he was long past being merely annoyed. He was angry and it showed.

"As I said before, Mr. McClain," she finally managed to snap, "you have to speak to these boys about their behavior! I've tried time and again, but nothing seems to work."

"That's enough!" Drew thundered, over the renewed hum of raised voices. "We can discuss that later and in private. Right now, I want to know what happened."

The crowd, busily exchanging comments about the explosion, stilled at the sound of his voice.

"Enough?" Leslie shouted, her face white with anger. "If you'd listened to me when I asked you the first time to keep an eye on the boys, this wouldn't have happened. Someone has to talk to them before they kill themselves and take someone with them!"

"She's right," a male voice behind Drew interjected. "Those kids of hers are terrors. It's not the first time they've stirred up trouble around here, either. If they're responsible for the explosion, someone in authority ought to do something about them. We have our businesses to think of."

"Businesses, Paul?" Maddie cast a cold look at Paul Stevens, the man who ran the small butcher shop. "Your place is more for show than profit and you know it. In fact, most of the businesses around here are run by retired people who enjoy living back in the nineteenth century, me included." She fixed the butcher with a cold look. "How come you aren't interested in knowing if anyone's been hurt?"

Stevens had the grace to look ashamed. "Hell, just look at those two kids—they're okay. And, plain as the nose on your face, they're responsible for whatever happened. They're damned lucky to be alive, I'd say!" the man muttered. A chorus of voices rose in agreement.

Drew glared at the grumbling assembly. "Let me

take care of this, Maddie. Now, the rest of you get back to what you were doing before the explosion.''

"Us, too?" Jeremy Chambers asked as he drew closer to his mother.

Drew, now that he was sure no one had been seriously injured, was prepared to be generous. But not yet, and not in plain sight. And not before the boy and his brother were made to realize the gravity of their "crime."

"No way. Not the two of you." Drew wiped his chin on a corner of the towel and frowned when he saw the streak of blood mingled with shaving cream. "Definitely, not you," he added firmly. "I want you to come with me."

"What are you going to do to us?" Tim whispered.

"Yes, what *are* you going to do?" Leslie echoed. At the look on Drew's face, for the first time, she began to wonder whether she was doing the right thing by asking him to do something about her children. Yet a shudder ran through her as she thought of what could have happened if luck hadn't been with the boys.

"Simple." Drew reached for the children's hands. "I'm taking them in for questioning."

"Questioning?" Leslie asked. "What more do you need to know than they were playing with a stick of dynamite in the gully behind my store? I'm fed up, I tell you," Leslie went on. "This is the last straw!"

"I play by the rules, Ms. Mayor," Drew answered once he had the boys firmly in his grip. "Everyone is innocent until he's proven guilty. I intend to listen to their story before I make up my mind. If they're behind this, you can rest assured they won't forget today in a hurry.''

"Fine with me! Whatever you do, just make it stick. I've tried every baby-sitter in the area to keep an eye on the boys this summer while I run my shop. None of them lasted more than a day or two.'' Her look of utter frustration was Drew's undoing.

He nodded curtly and headed for the jail before their mother could have second thoughts about giving the kids up to his tender mercies. As disgusted as he was with what the kids had evidently been up to, he noticed a look of apprehension pass over her face at the last minute.

Just what did she think he was going to do to them?

Too bad they didn't have a father around the house to teach them how far they could go and still be kids.

Not that he'd had a father figure himself who'd cared about the trouble Drew had gotten himself into. His uncle Thomas had made it clear when Drew's mother and father had died, within months of each other, that he was doing his duty just by taking in his sister's son. Even his aunt, decent woman that she was, had been too preoccupied with five younger children of her own to offer the attention a growing boy needed.

They'd fed and clothed him and seen to it he attended school. No more, no less. As far as he was concerned, it was that sterile upbringing that had made him roam restlessly around the country since he was seventeen, looking for something that would make him feel he belonged. Not that he knew just where or what it was. Only that it had to be out there, somewhere.

One thing was becoming clear. Whatever he was looking for, it was definitely not in Calico.

"OH, MADDIE, I'm not sure I've done the right thing." Leslie said as Maddie Hanks joined her. "Drew McClain looked awfully disgusted. What if he really plans some awful punishment for the boys?" Her voice trailed off as she gazed after the trio disappearing into the jail.

"Now, don't you worry, dear," Maddie reassured her. "Drew's a friend of the sheriff. He wouldn't have asked him to help out if he didn't think Drew was a decent man. I'm sure Drew would never do anything to harm those kids of yours. Probably just talk a little sense into them."

"It's just that I was finally at my wit's end," Leslie admitted, frustrated at the boys' latest escapade. "They have never done anything as dangerous as this before. You don't think he'll turn them over to the juvenile authorities in Barstow, do you?"

"No," Maddie answered. "Heck, they're only two little kids. He'll read them the riot act and let them go. You'll see."

"Fat lot of good that's going to do," Leslie answered somewhat contrarily. "I've done that myself—more times than I care to count." She sighed. "I think I'll go see what's going on."

Drew was pulling on his shirt when she entered the jail. A quick glance around for Jeremy and Tim came up empty. Until she noticed two still, small bodies topped with worried faces huddled together on a cot behind the bars of a cell.

"You're actually arresting them?" she asked.

"Sure," Drew replied as he finished tucking his shirt into his jeans. "I'm in charge here, or hadn't you noticed?" He motioned to a wooden chair alongside his desk. "Why don't you take a seat over there while I interrogate the suspects?"

Leslie's blood ran cold. She was frustrated over the boys' behavior, true, but she'd never thought Drew would go this far. "You're not going to turn them over to the juvenile authorities, are you?"

"Now, that's an interesting thought, but no, I'm not," he answered. "Seems to me, Ms. Mayor, that just a few minutes ago you asked me to do you a favor and put the fear of God into your children. Am I right?"

"Yes, but I never thought you'd actually lock them up like a couple of criminals!"

Drew regarded her for a moment, shrugged, sauntered over to the cell and pulled the door open.

"The door was never locked and they knew it," he answered. "They could have left at any time if they'd really wanted to. Right, boys?"

The boys nodded in unison. Jeremy, his cowlick hanging over his blue eyes, looked worried as he gazed at Drew. Tim, his cropped brown hair left standing straight up by the blast, had a tear or two rolling down his cheeks. Both sat rooted to the cot.

"I intended to have a man-to-man talk with them as soon as I finished dressing," Drew told Leslie, "but they can leave now, if that's what you want. Make up your mind, lady."

Leslie hesitated. *Man-to-man?* They were only children!

When she realized *she'd* been the one who had asked Drew to handle the boys, she was reminded of an old saying along the lines of *Be careful what you wish for, because you just might get it.*

She could see her boys were trying to keep a stiff upper lip as they and the deputy exchanged glances. A silent communication, obviously only known to males, passed between them. The fact that they didn't come charging out the door as soon as the deputy had opened it showed they respected his authority enough to wait for him to call the shots.

Drew McClain didn't know her boys as well as she did, Leslie thought glumly. They were always contrite and apologetic after getting into trouble. Not that that stopped them from heading into trouble again as soon as they thought up a new way of finding it. Still, she was only their mother. This man was a real sheriff with a badge. Maybe that would make a difference.

Well, she decided, as long as the boys seemed willing enough to stay put, she might as well leave the three of them together. At least, "the talk," if it took, would give her and the town a few days' respite.

"I'd rather leave the boys with you, if you don't mind. They don't seem to listen to a word I say— maybe they'll listen to you," she said in answer to McClain's questioning look. "As for you both," she added grimly to the wide-eyed boys, "I'll see you when you come home."

Drew waited until their mother was gone before he

entered the jail cell. He sat down on the cot opposite to the boys.

"Okay, fellows. We're going to do this by the book. What's your full name?" he asked Jeremy.

"Jeremy Chambers," the kid answered, trying to look nonchalant and only managing to look uneasy.

"You older than your brother?"

"Yeah, I'm ten."

"Yes, sir!" Drew corrected. One thing he intended was for the boys to learn a healthy respect for the law. He waited for a reluctant nod. "And you?" he asked Tim.

"Timothy Chambers, sir. I'm eight."

"Old enough to know better," Drew commented. The little guy was a quick study, thank goodness. "Didn't your dad ever teach you right from wrong?"

"We don't have a dad," Jeremy answered for his brother. "He went away a long time ago when we were real little and we haven't seen him since. He and Mom are divorced."

Drew felt a wave of sympathy for the two young miscreants. The way Jeremy and his brother spoke so matter-of-factly about being abandoned by their father would have been enough to soften any man—if it hadn't been for the danger the kids had placed themselves and others in.

"Seems to me both of you are old enough to realize you've been a pain in the neck to your mother and the whole town. You could have gotten yourselves killed," Drew said sternly. "Mind telling me what you two were doing out there?"

"We found an old stick of dynamite," Jeremy

started in, "and I just was wondering what would happen if..." Drew's raised eyebrows silenced him.

"And?" Drew prompted. "Then what?"

"We were throwing rocks at it to see if it would explode."

"Whose idea was that?"

"Mine, I guess," Jeremy answered slowly. "Don't blame Tim. He always does what I do."

"Do you ever stop to think what might happen to him and others because of your fool ideas?"

"No, sir. But no one got hurt." The expression on his face was hopeful.

Drew regarded him gravely. "Only by a miracle." He waited until his statement had a chance to sink in. "So, have you learned anything from this latest idea of yours?"

The kids looked at each other as if debating whether to put up a defense. "Guess so," Jeremy answered. Tim nodded his agreement.

"What?"

"Never throw rocks at dynamite?" Jeremy grinned hopefully.

"And what are you going to do if you find any more dynamite lying around?"

"Come and tell you?"

"Right," Drew agreed. "Learn anything else from all of this?"

"Try to stay out of trouble?" Tim ventured.

"Right, again," Drew replied, not that he believed it for a minute. "Now, it appears you're both guilty of malicious mischief. That's usually punishable by six months in jail," he added, tongue in cheek. "The question is, what kind of punishment fits this crime?'' he said thoughtfully.

Jeremy blinked. Tim gulped and moved closer to his brother.

"Now go on, get on home and get cleaned up," Drew told them. "I don't want to see you in here again. Got it?"

"Aren't you going to tell us what you're going to do to us?" Tim asked. "Mom always thinks of something." He jumped when his brother prodded him with an elbow.

Drew nodded, trying hard to keep a stern look on his face. "Yep, and so will I. For now, I'm going to remand you both into your mother's care. I'll be up to your house to discuss your punishment with you soon. In the meantime, don't leave the area unless I tell you to. Now get!"

"Yes, sir!" Jeremy made for the jailhouse door with his brother hard at his heels.

Drew stretched out on the cot as soon as he was alone. If the possible outcome of the kids' latest adventure hadn't been so potentially serious, he would have laughed out loud. Not because it was funny, but because the two reminded him of himself when he was a kid.

As a matter of fact, knowing from his own personal experience that "the talk" wasn't going to last for more than the time it took for the kids to come up with a new idea, he felt kind of sorry for Leslie Chambers. He knew, as sure as he knew his own name, it would just be a matter of time before he had those kids in here again. He sighed.

One thought led to another: Leslie's sparkling green eyes. Hair the color of a fading sunset. The trim figure a man's arms ached to hold. That is, if the man wasn't a traveling man, like himself.

He didn't know the reason behind her divorce from the kid's father, but he was willing to bet women like Leslie usually played for keeps.

MADDIE HEADED for the group of men standing in front of the saloon. "Well?" she demanded. "Haven't you fellows anything better to do than stand there and mind someone else's business?"

"Now, Maddie," Frank said. "We're just talking about the pool. After this morning, we've decided the odds against the mayor have gone up. The deputy's sure as hell going to tame her and her kids."

"That's what you think," Maddie snorted. "That woman has a backbone of steel and a brain in her head."

"So does the deputy." Elias laughed. "And I'm still betting on him. Raising the bet's fine with me. You haven't said anything to her, have you?"

"No. What do you mean, 'raising the bet'?" Maddie asked. "I'm the only one taking odds on Leslie! Don't I have a say in this?"

"Nah," Elias answered. "Do you want to stay in this pool or not?"

"Stay," Maddie answered grimly. "You're underestimating the power of a woman." She frowned at Elias. "The whole thing could turn into a draw, you know."

"What do you mean by that?"

"You'll see," Maddie answered gleefully, turning her back on the gaping men. She took a parting shot over her shoulder as she swung her frying pan and started to walk away. "Right now, I'm betting on Leslie, come hell or high water."

DREW WAITED just long enough for the kids to have a chance to think about what he'd told them before he set out for their mother's antique-quilt shop up the street. It was time to discuss her boys' punishment.

The post office, the barbershop and all the other small shops in between were open. Tourists were strolling the boardwalk. *Good,* Drew thought, as he tipped his Stetson to the ladies and nodded good morning to Peter Lord, the new owner of the apothecary shop. It was back to business as usual.

He took an appreciative look around as he entered the open door to Leslie Chambers's business enterprise, the Quilt Lady. The clean odor of new materials and the scent of potpourri filled the single large room. Counters were piled high with bolts of colorful cloth, rolls of batting. A glass showcase sheltered rows of matching threads, needles, pins and gadgets Drew assumed were needed to make a quilt. A rack held books and quilt patterns. Antique quilts hung on the walls. Open for inspection, newer quilts were displayed neatly on a counter. Country music came from the CD player.

Leslie sat bending over an unfinished quilt stretched on a wooden frame, silently making tiny stitches. She'd changed into a fresh period costume whose bodice had been shaped to her exquisite figure. A fresh ribbon was entwined in her French braid. He could see the tip of a delicate slipper peeking out from under her skirt. Her foot tapped in time to the music.

He watched her worry her lower lip as she pushed the needle in and out with quick, determined stitches. Her rigid posture and clenched lips spoke louder than words: the lady was still mad as hell.

With difficulty, he tore his eyes away from Leslie, cleared his throat and looked around the store for her sons. He had more important things to do than stand there and gawk at a pretty woman, like a schoolboy.

The boys were nowhere in sight.

One thing was clear, it had taken less than one hour for the boys to forget he'd ordered them to wait at home for him. A record even he had never dared to equal when he was their age and waiting for his punishment.

Leslie raised her head at the interruption. The deputy stood silently regarding her. She couldn't quite make out what was behind the frown on his face but the truth was, even as she resented having come to him with her problems, she owed him. The least she could do was be polite.

"Hello," she said as she forced a smile on her face. She rose, straightened her rumpled skirt down over her legs and came forward.

"I've come to tell the kids what their punishment will be, just as promised."

"Yes, of course," she answered as she came toward him. "Thank you for taking the trouble."

"You're welcome." He glanced away from the worried look in her eyes. "So this is where you spend your time?"

"Yes," she answered with a tight smile. "When I'm not busy trying to keep an eye on the boys."

"Got a few minutes to talk?"

"Yes, of course," she answered. "By the way, whatever you told the boys seems to have sunk in. They've been awfully quiet since they came home. I guess I should thank you for helping with them—I worry about them so much."

Drew raised his eyebrows. He was glad to see she hadn't given up on her kids. They deserved to have at least one parent who cared about them. "As far as I'm concerned," he remarked dryly, "when boys like yours become quiet, it's time to worry. Where are the kids, anyway?"

Leslie gestured to the door at the rear of the shop. "Out back, picking up pieces of the porch railing."

"Good. That ought to keep them busy for a while."

With a frown, Leslie went to the back door and called to Jeremy and Tim. If what the deputy had said was correct, she thought with a sinking feeling, it *was* time to worry. The boys *had* been quieter than usual. Was it too much to hope for that they'd learned a lesson on responsibility, after all?

"Well, boys, I'm here as promised," Drew announced when the youngsters came into the store, dragging their feet, and stopped in front of him. He waited until he had their and their mother's full attention. "Here's what I've decided is going to be your punishment. Ready?"

With a sidelong glance at their mother, the boys nodded.

"One. You're going to apologize to everyone you

meet from now on for the trouble you've been causing around here.''

Leslie looked pleased. The boys looked as though they'd swallowed lemons.

"Two," Drew continued, "you're going to sweep every sidewalk in town once a day for a week."

"What kind of punishment do you call that?" Leslie asked curiously.

"It's called community service," Drew answered as if daring her to disagree. "Seems to me the kids owe it to the town after messing it up."

Leslie nodded her agreement. "I guess the punishment should fit the crime."

"Right. Oh, and yes, there's one more item." He turned back to the boys. "You're going to rebuild your mother's back porch."

At first, the boys had looked relieved at their relatively mild punishment. Now they looked surprised. Drew managed to keep a straight face.

"How are we going to do that?"

"Easy," Drew replied. "With wood, nails, a hammer and a lot of hard work. It'll help get rid of all that extra energy you don't seem to know what to do with."

"I really don't think the boys are capable of repairing the porch railing," Leslie interjected. "For one thing, it's in pieces. Aside from that, I'm sure they wouldn't even know where to start. I think it's a job for a grown man."

"Easy," Drew replied. "I'm going to show them how."

From the look on Leslie's face, he knew she was

taken aback by his statement. Hell, for that matter, he was as surprised by his impulsive offer as she was.

The decision to have the boys repair the porch railing had been made in a split second. The offer to help them had taken even less time.

And all because Leslie Chambers had smiled and thanked him for doing something his badge and his oath of office required him to do.

Or maybe it had been the charming sight of her bending over her quilting, her long red hair braided with a blue ribbon to match the bodice of the pretty blue dress she wore. And the sudden realization that, temper aside, she was a fascinating woman. He needed a valid reason to spend more time in her company.

Ice lady be damned, Drew thought as he told the boys he'd see them tomorrow. He'd been around enough to recognize a red-blooded woman when he saw one.

Chapter Three

What did the mayor want now?

Drew crumpled the "Meet me in the town hall" message. He might be attracted to Leslie, but he didn't like being ordered around. Not by her, not by anyone. A glance outside the door told him that, whatever problem had come up, at least it wasn't about the kids.

He'd personally seen to it their apologies were made before he'd placed them on their honor and left them sweeping the boardwalks. In fact, he could see the two of them now, industriously sweeping in front of the jail and working their way to the Last Chance.

So far, so good.

He didn't have to guess what was going to happen next. Sure as shootin', Maddie Hanks would be out there with glasses of lemonade and sweet talk to ease the boys' labors.

Normally, he wouldn't have thought twice about the "invitation." After all, he was only passing through on his way to who-knows-where. But the town's new lady mayor had managed to pique his interest in a way no other woman had ever done before now. Not only because of her good looks, although Lord knew she had more than enough to interest any man. Maybe it was because he was drawn to her spunk and an even larger measure of spice.

That, and those luscious lips that ached to be kissed.

Together, they all spelled trouble.

He'd heard enough about Leslie Chambers by now to suspect she was a woman who tried to be in control of her life, her kids and her surroundings. And to learn that she'd frozen out three-quarters of the eligible males in Calico. How she was able to handle the job of managing a reconstructed ghost town that had a reputation of not being interested in being managed was another story.

Maybe now would be as good a time as any to drop in on the mayor and begin to discover what made her tick, he decided as he unfolded and studied the message. And, while he was at it, in spite of the fact they were obviously incompatible, he might find out exactly what it was about her that made him entertain thoughts of hanging around Calico long enough to find out the answer.

He put what could be politely termed an invitation in the back pocket of his worn jeans and headed out to do some research.

Sure enough, the Chambers kids were seated on a bench in front of the Last Chance, drinking lemonade. A fast-disappearing plate of cookies sat between them. In the bright morning sunlight, the boys looked deceptively like two little innocent angels.

Drew knew better. In fact, judging from the way Jeremy was thoughtfully studying his surroundings,

Drew suspected the kid was dreaming up some new way to bedevil the town.

As soon as he took care of Leslie, Drew intended to get the kids started on repairing the railing on the back porch of their mother's shop. In fact, he thought wryly as he waved to them and headed for the new town hall, he was actually looking forward to making himself useful by tackling the repair job himself.

Who was he kidding? he thought ruefully as he strode up the street. It wasn't the carpentry job at Leslie Chambers's shop that interested him. Replacing the railing would give him an excuse to see more of her—but on his terms. Not that they were particularly friendly at the moment. Their relationship was more like an armed truce. The last thing he wanted was to start another war.

The ramshackle building that had become the town hall had been recently painted. He glanced up at the new sign above the door: Town Hall, Calico, California, 1880. The building was actually well over one hundred years old. Like the rest of the town, it managed to retain the aura of its past.

With a glance over his shoulder to make sure the boys had gone back to sweeping, Drew entered the building.

The small hall was dominated by the customary flag of the United States and the Bear flag of the State of California. At the rear, there was a door labeled Gents, and a recently added Ladies. The odor of new paint and freshly sawed wood permeated the room. A dozen new pine benches were lined up in front of the slicked-up bar.

A bar?

Drew stopped in his tracks and took a second look. Surely the mayor didn't intend to conduct the meeting from behind the bar?

He turned around when he heard footsteps. It was Leslie, all dolled up in the latest mid-nineteenth-century fashions from the top of her bonneted auburn hair to her trim, booted feet. As eye-catching as she appeared in her costume, he still wondered just what she would have looked like in the jeans he'd glimpsed under her dress the other day. His body tightened when he visualized snug jeans and a T-shirt that most certainly would have hugged her lush breasts.

"Well, here I am," he said casually, trying to channel his thoughts to a safer subject. "Whatever you have to say, make it quick. I'm busy."

Leslie eyed him carefully. Her raised eyebrows told him she knew he was lying. Calico, still a sleepy town on the verge of awakening for the tourist season, required little of him. No matter. He didn't intend to stick around any longer than it took to hear what it was that had riled her up this time.

When she didn't reply right away, he took the opportunity to gaze around the room. In spite of having been obviously refurbished, it still looked like a saloon. "Where are you planning on conducting business?"

"Over there." Leslie gestured to where a high stool had been placed behind the bar. On the wall behind it hung an enormous painting of a buxom, nude woman with a flimsy scarf appropriately draped over private places.

"You intend to run the meeting from the bar?"

"Why not?" she asked. "At least that way I'll be assured of getting everyone's attention while I conduct business."

She was only half right, Drew mused as he studied the painting. No doubt everyone's attention would be focused on the bar, but her audience would probably be ogling the painting instead of listening to her. And waiting for her to serve up drinks.

Drew shrugged. "Whatever works, I guess," he muttered as he surveyed the newly refurbished room. "Anyway, the place looks good."

"And it was all done with volunteer help," Leslie added proudly.

"Volunteer?" He couldn't see any of the men he'd met around Calico volunteering to lift anything more than a cold glass of beer. Certainly nothing that might work up an ounce of sweat. For the most part, they were too busy playacting. As far as he could tell, if it weren't for the six-dollar entry price of admission to the town itself, Calico would have gone broke long ago.

"Yes, volunteer," Leslie answered sweetly. "Everyone was told they had to provide his or her labor or pay to have someone else come to town to take care of it. I'm happy to say they chose the former."

"Volunteer, my eye," Drew remarked with a shrug. "Why don't you call it what is was, blackmail?"

She smiled.

"If you keep up those tactics, Ms. Mayor," Drew added dryly, "the good citizens of Calico might change their minds about wanting local government and the law and order that goes with it."

"Not at all," she assured him. "It was just the opposite. In fact, there have been so many visitors recently to Calico, everyone, including me, saw the need for some kind of local government. That's how I became mayor. By the way, I was the one who requested the county sheriff to hire someone as part of that plan. We've never had a deputy sheriff around here before now." She eyed him speculatively. "We're still waiting to see how you work out."

So she was the one who had arranged to have him hired, Drew thought grimly. Considering that it was her kids who were causing the only problems in town, he could understand her request for some kind of law. Too bad it had to be him. As he returned her steady gaze, he still wasn't all sure just how grateful he ought to be.

"What was it you needed me for this time?" he inquired.

"We're having our first town hall meeting tomorrow night," she answered.

"So?"

"So, I asked you here so we could talk privately and to make certain you would attend and looked decent."

"Decent?" Drew hurriedly checked his zipper.

"For one thing, you haven't shaved."

"I was about to when I got your message," he answered, starting to be annoyed as hell. "I didn't have time."

"And you need to be dressed properly," she added.

Dressed properly? Drew's temper rose by ninety degrees as he gazed at her incredulously. "What's wrong with what I'm wearing now?"

"Nothing, if you're living in the late twentieth century," she answered, "but here in Calico we're living in the nineteenth." Leslie eyed the worn jeans that fit him better than they should have for her peace of mind. And the short-sleeved T shirt that covered his muscular chest and little else. Both were undoubtedly comfortable in the desert heat, but his body was playing havoc with her senses.

And he certainly didn't look like a lawman.

"As mayor, I want to see everyone acting the part and dressed accordingly. The point is," she hurried on, "you need to be in costume while you're here in Calico. I'd recommend Levi's with a belt that has a large western buckle. And a decent checkered cotton shirt and bolo tie. I'd like to see you look as if you're living in 1881!"

"You what?" His question sounded ominous, but she didn't care.

"You heard me!" Leslie answered, her own temper rising to match his. After all, as far as she was concerned, she wasn't being unreasonable. "And furthermore—" she pointed to his argyle socks "—those have to go!"

"That tears it," Drew muttered as he returned her gaze. Sometimes, he knew, the only way to silence an irate woman was to kiss her speechless. Impulsively, he gave in to an urge he'd had from the first time he'd met her and managed to suppress until now.

Without another word, he grabbed her by the shoulders, pulled her to his chest and lowered his lips to hers. Soft, honeyed lips, he thought dimly as he deepened his kiss. Just as he'd suspected they would be.

Taken by surprise, Leslie struggled in his arms. Until she realized the demanding lips meeting hers were sending pleasurable electric shocks throughout her. Instinctively, she relaxed against him, and, for the quick moment, savored the pressure of his hard, muscular chest against her breasts.

Unbidden thoughts surged through her mind. It had been three long years since she'd been held by a man. And she certainly had never been kissed the way Drew was kissing her, or she'd have remembered. When she found herself surrendering to the pressure of his mouth against hers, she pulled away and held her fingers to her bruised lips. "What do you think you're doing?" she gasped.

"Damned if I know," he replied, looking just as surprised as she was.

Appalled at her response to him, Leslie stared at Drew. Maybe she'd been wrong to ask the sheriff to hire a deputy in the first place. Drew had not only become a threat to her peace of mind, she was afraid he'd just started something she had no intention of finishing. And certainly not with a wandering man. One such man in her life was more than enough.

"Well, good luck with your meeting tomorrow night," he finally muttered as he turned to leave.

"Do you plan on being here?"

"I don't think so," he answered. He'd be damned if he'd dress up in some silly costume just to please her. "I signed up to help keep the peace, not to be an actor. Besides, it depends," he threw back over his shoulder.

"Depends? On what?"

"How well your kids manage to stay out of trouble. I might be otherwise occupied."

He smiled his satisfaction when he heard her outraged gasp, then he strode out the swinging doors and let them bang shut behind him. That ought to show her he wasn't going to let her push him around.

The sun was standing straight up—high noon. It was time to check on those kids of hers. He shaded his eyes and looked around for Jeremy and Tim and saw them coming out of the saloon up the street, each carrying a stack of what appeared to be red posters.

The saloon? When his sixth sense began to peal like crazy, Drew headed straight for the boys before they could contrive to get away from him.

"Finished sweeping?" he asked. They nodded, but from the guilty look on their faces, Drew sensed something was up. "Mind telling me what you were doing inside the saloon?"

Jeremy, strangely speechless for once, seemed to draw a blank. Tim took a step backward and pulled on his brother's shirttail. Jeremy shook him off.

Drew almost groaned when he recalled the thoughtful look on Jeremy's face earlier that morning. That alone should have alerted him to trouble coming full steam around the bend. Sure as hell, the kids had been into or up to some mischief.

Resigned to the probability he wasn't going to like Jeremy's answer, Drew quickly came to the point. "You might as well tell me now," he invited. "I'll find out anyway."

"We were distributing handbills," Jeremy answered, managing to avoid looking him straight in the eyes.

"Handbills?" Drew started to relax. Until he caught the quick look Jeremy exchanged with his brother. "The one advertising the meeting at the town hall tomorrow night?"

"Not exactly," Jeremy answered, swatting at Tim's clutching hand.

"So, what, exactly?" Drew asked as he reached for the stack of bright red papers.

Jeremy blinked, drew in his breath and with a warning glance at his brother, relinquished the handbills.

Drew stiffened as he read. The handbills were red flags, and his reaction to them the same as that of a bull he'd once encountered when he was riding the rodeo circuit.

REWARD, it read. For the Right Man, Who Will Marry Our Mother and Be Our Dad. It was signed Jeremy and Timothy Chambers.

"Who printed these up for you?" Drew demanded when he could breathe normally.

"Mr. Strawberry. He's the one who prints the Calico Gazette."

"Why?" Drew shot back.

"Because we paid him five dollars to do it." The kids took a backward step at his reaction.

"And the reward?" Drew asked cautiously. "Just what kind of reward are you talking about?"

"Twenty dollars. We saved up twenty-five," Jeremy added bravely, "but after we paid for the handbills, that's all we have left."

"And you think that's enough money to tempt some man to ask your mother to marry him?"

"Not just any man," Jeremy explained. "We both have to like him. After all, he's going to be our dad."

A dad!

Drew's anger faded as he pretended to study the handbill. It was obvious the boys were desperate to have a father back in their lives, but they had been going about it the wrong way. No wonder half the people in town were leery of their mother and the other half just plain disgusted with her kids.

He didn't know what kind of a man their father had been before he'd disappeared, but it was obvious the kids missed having a father all the same. With a pang, Drew remembered how much he'd missed his own parents after he'd lost them in an automobile accident. And he remembered the stupid things he'd done out of sheer anger at being left alone.

He was honest enough to admit he'd been a living example of how easy it was for a boy to lose his way without a father's influence.

His heart ached for the kids. If only there was some way he could bring their father back to them, he would.

But he also knew all hell would break loose if their mother heard about her sons' latest escapade.

At any rate, he thought dryly, this new idea of theirs was probably better than their earlier plan to kidnap some man and get him to marry their mother. That is, if that's what Leslie was talking about when she'd first cornered him for help. Not much better, but some. At least this one was legal.

"Tell you what," he said as he stuffed the remainder of the handbills in his pocket. "Let's see if we can retrieve the ones you've already distributed. We wouldn't want your mother to get wind of this, would we?''

Jeremy silently stared at him before he nodded.

"Okay. Jeremy, you go on down the street and get back the handbills you've already passed out. Tim, you wait here. I'll retrieve the ones you left inside.''

As soon as Drew's eyes adjusted to the dim interior of the saloon, he knew he was too late. A small knot of men was gathered in a corner looking at one of the handbills and laughing.

Laughing?

What was there about Leslie Chambers that would set the men to laughing at the idea of marrying her?

He heard Tim creep up behind him. "Maybe we ought to forget it,'' the kid whispered. "It's too late, anyway.''

"It's never too late to right a wrong, Tim,'' Drew replied. "It's all in the way you go about it.''

He sauntered toward the group. "Just a misguided joke, gentlemen,'' he said as he came alongside Keith Andrews, the local tintype portrait photographer. "Looks as if the kids got a little carried away, doesn't it?''

"Hell, it's worth thinking about,'' Andrews replied, studying the red handbill. "Especially when there's a reward attached to the offer.'' He glanced speculatively at Tim peeking around Drew. "How big a reward, kid?''

"Really big,'' said Tim proudly. "Bigger than anybody can imagine.''

Drew put a restraining hand on him. "There is no

reward. None," he articulated clearly. "I thought I just told you, it was a joke."

"Joke? The only part of the joke is expecting someone to be willing to marry the kid's mother," Herb Strawberry interjected. "She's told off every man in sight ever since she settled here two years ago."

"You included?" Drew asked softly.

Strawberry flushed. The group of men around him snickered.

"Is that why you printed up the handbill for the kids?" Drew asked. "To get even with Leslie Chambers?"

Strawberry drew himself up to his full height, all five feet six inches. "I'll have you know I'm a professional man. Printing handbills is part of my business."

"Then I suggest you be more circumspect about what you print in the future," Drew replied.

"How about the reward, or maybe even the bet?" Keith Andrews persisted. His eyes narrowed as his gaze flickered from Drew to Tim and back before he remarked slyly, "What's going on? Trying to get in good with the kids so you can get everything for yourself?"

Drew barely managed to control himself. He reached for the handbill. "You'd never believe the truth if I told it to you," he answered. "In the meantime, why don't you just forget you ever saw this."

"No way," Andrews replied. "It's my property now."

"Suit yourself," Drew answered. "But if you do anything to upset Ms. Chambers, you'll have to answer to me," he warned. "Got it?" He gazed at Andrews so coolly that Andrews's complexion turned a shade or two pinker. Drew took Tim by the hand and started for the saloon's swinging doors.

"Forget the reward! When hell freezes over," Keith Andrews exploded behind him. "Who does he think he is, anyway?"

"The guy who's going to tame our mayor, that's who," a voice answered. "One way or another. Maybe he even wants her for himself. As a matter of fact, I think I'll bet a bundle on him. Here, who's holding the pool? I want to increase my bet."

Drew, overhearing this exchange, had paused at the door. Tame Leslie Chambers? Pool? Bet?

"Forget the bet," Andrews announced defiantly. "I'm going after Leslie. The mayor isn't half bad-looking, at that. Besides, I always thought there was a good chance there'd be a vein of silver running through that property of hers. Before I'm through with her, it's going to be mine."

Drew was tempted to turn back and teach Andrews a lesson the braggart would never forget. He told himself it was because the fool had no respect for Leslie either as a woman or as the town's mayor. As for a vein of silver, the records he'd seen in Barstow showed any trace of silver had long since been mined out.

But it was more than that. Andrews had managed to touch a nerve. Drew's own feelings about Leslie Chambers were mixed, at best, running from hot to just plain mad. But one thing he was sure of—no one was going to talk about her that way, in a saloon or anyplace else. Not while he was around to stop it.

He hesitated, and looked down at Tim's drawn face,

where tears threatened to flow. He changed his mind. Whatever stupidity was going on back there involving himself and Leslie or Andrews would have to wait until he was alone. Right now he had two kids to worry about. Two kids who wanted a father so badly they were ready to resort to any scheme to get one.

He put a sympathetic hand on Tim's slight shoulder and felt him tremble. Drew gave him a reassuring squeeze. "Everything's going to be okay," he told him. "You have my word on it."

As for himself, now that he knew what was going on around town, he sure as hell wasn't stupid enough to allow himself to be bought, fired or for that matter, kidnapped, if what Leslie had said when she'd tried to hire him was true.

Thank goodness he was the new man on the block and the kids were too much in awe of him to consider him a candidate in their search for a father.

"McCLAIN, YOU HAVE TO DO something about those kids!" Alan Little, the irate stable owner shouted as he came through the front door of the jail.

"What kids?"

"Those Chambers boys, that's who!"

"What's the matter now?" Drew asked. "Don't you like the way they're whitewashing the toolshed out back?"

"Whitewashing, my eye," Little thundered. "They've just ridden off with two of my best livestock! I want you to bring the horses back before those kids injure them!"

Drew sighed. He'd put the boys to work while he

prepared to go for supplies to repair the porch railing. He'd even convinced himself the boys had learned their lesson yesterday, and two days before, for that matter. He should have known better.

He cast a longing glance at the hearty lunch Maddie had sent over from the Last Chance. There was no telling when he'd get to eat if he left now.

"So, what are you waiting for?" The livery stable owner glowered, his face mottled with anger. "I want those horses returned. The sooner, the better!"

"Keep your shirt on," Drew replied. "Let me get my gear." He reached for the lunch tray, intending to pocket a sandwich.

The door to the jail banged open. Drew paused, his hand outstretched.

"Hurry! I just saw my boys heading for the hills on horses!" Leslie Chambers shouted between gasps for air. "We have to go after them before they get hurt!"

"Tell me about it," Drew muttered, forgetting the ham sandwich. He opened the desk drawer and took out the keys to his Land Rover. "I was just leaving."

"Good, I'll come with you," Leslie announced.

"No. You go on home and wait in case they come back," Drew told her. "I don't need help in bringing back two little kids. They couldn't have gone very far."

"I don't care, I'm going with you to make sure the boys aren't hurt. Don't forget, I'm their mother."

Her flushed face and flashing eyes reminded Drew of her reaction after their kiss. Frustrated with himself for thinking of honeyed lips at a time like this, he made for the door.

"Going after those two 'horse thieves' is part of my job," Drew repeated. "I told you, I don't need any help."

"Horse thieves?" Leslie turned pale. "Now I *know* I'm coming with you."

"No, you're not!" Drew answered. "Alan, see to it that Leslie gets home okay. I'll be back as soon as I find the boys."

Drew brushed past her and headed out into the rolling hills whose variegated shades of rose and lavender gave Calico its name. Twenty minutes later, all he could see were vast empty spaces with occasional small cave-like openings in the hills. He'd been told some were entrances to mines gone dry. Others had actually been miners' homes. There were so many, he didn't know where to start looking.

He stopped to think.

What would he have done if he'd been a kid looking for adventure?

DREW SLOWED when he came across an old miner's shack that had been built in front of an abandoned mine. The mine's opening had been boarded up, but several of the weathered boards had been pried loose and were lying on the ground.

The answer to his question became clear when he recognized Leslie's ancient automobile parked in front of the shack. He cursed silently when he realized she'd ignored his orders. He could have saved his breath.

Fearful that the boys, or even Leslie, might have fallen into the mine and were injured, he brought his vehicle to a stop. He'd start with the shack.

There were three sets of human footprints in the dust in front of the shack's door and a trail of horse's hoofprints. He glanced cautiously around, but there was no sign of a living thing.

"Damn the woman," he muttered while his heart pounded a mile a minute. She was no better at following orders than her kids. No wonder they behaved the way they did. Now he not only had the boys to worry about, he had Leslie's welfare on his mind as well.

He took his flashlight out of the car and headed for the shack. He tried the door. It was stuck.

"It's me, Drew McClain," he shouted to reassure anyone who might be inside. "I've come to help."

He turned on the flashlight and threw his shoulder against the door, which creaked open. Cautiously, he stepped inside. Before he knew what hit him, a form hurtled at him, almost knocking him to the ground. He ducked and raised his hands to protect himself.

"Thank goodness you came," Leslie cried as she threw herself into his arms. "I was afraid I was never going to be able to get out of here!"

Drew tried to soothe her while he glanced over her shoulder. In view of her distress, it was no time for lectures. "Are the boys with you?"

"No," she sobbed. "There were horses out front when I arrived, but Jeremy and Tim weren't inside when I looked." Her voice choked. "The door slammed shut before I could leave. I'm alone."

Drew heard a sound behind him. Before he had a chance to react, the door to the shack quietly closed. Outside, there was the sound of a bar falling into place.

"What the hell!" Drew threw his shoulder against

the door—this time it was closed for good. Calling for help was useless. In an abandoned shack in the middle of a desert, there was no one around to hear him. Except for whoever had locked him and Leslie inside. With a sinking feeling, he began to have an idea of just who the "whoever" might be.

He used his flashlight to survey the small one-room shack. The walls were covered with tar paper, with only one tiny cracked window high up. A lopsided table stood in the center of the room, and in addition, the shack held a single chair, a narrow cot with a thin, folded blanket and a lone pillow. On the table, someone had left bottled water, several cans of orange juice, a couple of apples and a bag of cookies. A kid's idea of nutrition.

It was clear that whoever had lured him and Leslie into the shack had planned it well in advance.

The more he thought about it, the clearer it became.

He didn't have to see the look on Leslie's face to realize that not only had he underestimated the determination of her kids to get a father for themselves, *he'd* also been had.

He'd been taken by two kids who might be half as tall as he was, but were twice as smart.

Chapter Four

Drew swore softly under his breath. How in blazes had he let himself be deliberately drawn to an abandoned shack, let alone be trapped inside with Leslie?

The shack was maybe eight by ten feet. He glanced again at the window overhead. It was a foot square, with four small murky panes. Even if the window could be opened, which he doubted, he'd never fit through. And, slight though she was, neither would Leslie.

He sank to his knees and shone the flashlight on the shack's foundation. Wooden boards had been hammered together with rusty nails. He couldn't pry the boards loose with his bare hands without flirting with blood poisoning. The only air in the shack came from narrow cracks around the door. Too narrow to get a decent grip.

He shuddered as he rose to his feet and brushed spiderwebs away from his shoulders. The odor of years of neglect and the dust rising from the dirt floor were overwhelming. Small footprints led to and from the rickety table, chair and cot. If anyone had lived in the shack recently, there was no real evidence of their presence.

He glanced at Leslie. She was shaking the latch on the door as though she could somehow force it open. When she saw him watching, she grimaced and wrapped her arms around herself for comfort. Despite the fire in her eyes, she looked cold and miserable. Shock, disbelief and anger passed across her face. As far as he could tell in the dim light of his flashlight, she didn't look comforted at the realization that, though she was locked up in a deserted, tar-papered miner's shack, she wasn't alone.

Not that he blamed her. He wasn't feeling too happy about the way things were going himself.

He'd quickly passed the shock and disbelief stage. His anger was simmering just below the surface. In fact, he was ready to blow his top at his own stupidity. The only thing that kept him from losing his cool was the knowledge it wasn't going to do one damned bit of good.

"Are you going to be okay?" he asked as he became aware of Leslie's abject misery.

"I've felt better," she answered. "Right now, I'm too furious to think straight. But when I get out of here, I'm going to blister the boys' hides. They won't be able to sit down for a week by the time I get through with them!"

Drew didn't blame her. She was fighting mad, but it was a hell of a lot better than crying over the kids. As he watched her try to collect herself, he could think of a dozen ways to show the boys the error of their ways—big time. It was a good thing they weren't handy.

Seething with frustration, he paced the rim of the

small room, searching for some way out. Short of knocking down a wall, it wasn't as easy as it looked. Whoever had built the shack had meant for it to last. He and Leslie were trapped.

In spite of his anger, he had to give the kids credit for their ingenuity. He studied the food on the table, the narrow cot, the single blanket. It looked as if the room had been set up for a singularly appealing scenario. Drew felt a moment's uncertainty. Were the kids old enough to have been thinking what *he* was thinking?

He glanced over at Leslie. She looked colder and more miserable than ever. His own anger had to take a back seat. At the moment, she needed comfort more than he needed to be plotting revenge. He considered how best to soothe her. Hold her? Kiss her? Something to take her mind off their unexpected captivity.

Maybe not. Not after the continued differences of opinion between them.

He eyed her warily. "It looks as if we're going to be roommates for a while."

"Roommates? That's not what I'd call being locked up against my will. Prisoners is more like it. Besides, how can you joke at a time like this?" she demanded. "Not only are we locked up in this forsaken place, it'll be dark soon and the boys could be out there in the desert alone. Maybe they're in trouble!"

"I have my doubts about that," Drew answered with a shrug as he eyed the bolted door. "If your kids were able to cook up this plan on such short notice, I'm sure they're smart enough to take care of themselves."

"What makes you think the boys are behind this?"

"Who else?" Drew asked dryly. "Although I wouldn't have believed they were capable of dreaming up this scenario if I weren't living it. I've been through oddball circumstances you'd probably find it hard to believe, but this is one I could have lived without."

The look passing over her face as she realized he was right was gratifying, but didn't do a damn thing to make him feel better about the mess they were in.

"Though I hate to admit it," he went on, "I have been caught off guard a few times in my life. But never before this way and by a ten-year-old and his eight-year-old brother."

He cast a jaundiced look at the food on the table. He'd not only missed lunch, it looked as if he wasn't going to have much of a dinner. Apples and cookies weren't enough to make a dent in his man-sized appetite. Too bad he hadn't taken the sandwich Maddie had sent over with him. He was starved.

"Look, there's a note on the table!" Leslie rushed to pick up an envelope under the bag of cookies. She blushed as she read the contents.

"It had better be good news. In fact, it had better be a clue as to how we get out of here," Drew said grimly as he reached over her shoulder for the note.

"I'm afraid it only says the boys are home asleep and will come for us in the morning."

"Asleep, hah!" Drew replied, as he studied the grimy note, realizing just what had made Leslie blush. "As for our getting to know each other..." His voice drifted off. If what he thought was behind the kidnapping was correct, the kids were matchmaking.

"They're probably staying up all night planning step two of their campaign."

"I don't understand," Leslie replied as she gazed around worriedly. "What do you suppose they mean by step two?"

Drew considered her question. He didn't intend to give away the kid's handbill caper unless he had to, but the answer to what was supposed to happen next was obvious. At least, to him. Even to Leslie, he was sure once she'd simmered down and accepted the situation.

"Simple. They figure if we get to know each other, maybe we'll decide to get married. That way, they'll have the dad they've been looking for."

"A dad?" Leslie forgot her discomfort. She shuddered as she slowly realized that Drew was right. This was exactly what the boys had had in mind with this foolishness. Hadn't she heard them planning the kidnapping just the other day? Now, in spite of her warning and Drew's attention, the kids had gone from talking about kidnapping a man and getting him to ask her to marry him to actually putting the plan into practice!

But Drew McClain!

He was the last man on earth she would ever consider as husband material. Not when he was an avowed wanderer, here today and planning to be gone tomorrow.

"How could the boys have managed to cook up a scheme like this without me knowing it?" she wondered aloud as she fought down a large dose of guilt. As the boys' mother, she should have made a greater effort to understand them, to reason with them, instead of asking Drew to straighten them out.

"You'll have to ask your ten-year-old if you want an answer to that question," Drew answered. "I'm a grown man, and *I* wouldn't have thought of this." He glanced around the one-room shack. "No, not in a dozen years."

Leslie glanced sharply at Drew. He was a grown man, all right. With cropped brown hair and hazel eyes, he was devastatingly handsome. His rugged figure had been honed to perfection by a life-style that had left no room for softness. And, to add to his attraction, every inch of him radiated an innate sensuality.

She bit her lower lip. Now was no time to be thinking of things that could only lead her into more trouble than she already had.

His eyes met hers. For a split second, she could have sworn a hint of a wicked smile had crossed his face. If she hadn't known better, she would have said there had even been a glimmer of interest in his eyes.

Her body tingled at the thought. Was she really attracted to him, she wondered, or was she so shaken by today's events that she needed the comfort of another adult human being? Especially one like Drew.

An inner warning filled her as she fought for a flip answer. But she couldn't think of a thing that made sense. Not when there wasn't anything flip about her reaction to him. And, from the look on his face, he recognized what was happening to her as well as she did.

A hunger she'd put behind her caught her unawares. It wasn't as if she hadn't known sexual desire before—

she'd been married for six contented years before her ex-husband, Walt, had turned forty and decided that life was passing him by. She'd been unable to trust a man since the day he'd walked out on her for another woman. Until Drew, she'd never met another man who had even tempted her to try.

Which didn't speak too well for her choices in men.

His utter maleness attracted her, but his personality still disturbed her. How could she be attracted to a man who had itchy feet?

She felt a curiosity, a heat, a tenseness in her middle. She looked away, anywhere but at Drew. Her glance fell on the narrow cot with its single pillow. She felt herself blush and hastily looked away. Right into his somber gaze.

"So, it's on to the step two the boys had in mind," he began.

"Drew, I can't... And certainly not at a time like this."

"Whatever you're going to say, hold on to it for a minute," he answered. He put the note and the flashlight on the table and gently pulled her to him.

He caught her chin with his fingertips, urged her face up to meet his lips, and kissed her before she could stop him. To her surprise, his hands were gentle and, in spite of the cold that filled the room, his lips were soft and warm. In seconds, she forgot he was a man she shouldn't trust, a man who kissed her passionately, but who might not want more than one night together. She drew back, trying to read his expression in the dim light.

"You read the note," Drew commented softly

against her throat. "It seems to me it's time for us to move on to the next stage."

His lips found hers again. She trembled as his kiss deepened, his embrace tightened. She couldn't move, speak, do anything more than lean into the arms that held her. And savor the pressure of his mouth on hers.

He was a man she'd only known for a few days, yet, incredibly, he'd made her forget everything but the arms that held her, the lips that caressed her. If only she could let herself return his kiss, could feel, taste, touch him the way he had touched her. She couldn't— not without opening herself to more heartache.

"You're lovely, Leslie Chambers," he murmured as his hands softly stroked the nape of her neck, moved down her back, all the while caressing her gently. "I can't imagine why the kids thought they had to find a husband for you. Surely, you must have attracted dozens of men in the past few years."

"Maybe," she answered as she pulled out of his arms. She felt a blush beginning to rise over her face. "But none I could trust, let alone love."

She glanced at the narrow cot and hurriedly looked away. "I don't think this is actually what the boys had in mind when they spoke of step two. I'm sure they only wanted us to get to know each other."

"It's as good a way as any I know of to get to know each other," Drew answered. He searched her eyes, saw her uncertainty reflected there. Reluctantly, he let her go.

"To be frank," she said agitatedly, moving out of his reach, "the little I do know about you scares me."

"What could there possibly be about me that scares

you?'' Drew asked. If he scared her, the vein pulsating at the side of her neck and her flushed face told him it wasn't in the normal ways. Unless he missed his guess, she was as moved by their brief embrace as he was.

''I told you my ex-husband walked out on us,'' Leslie began. ''Walt thought he was missing out on something. Not that he seemed to know what the something was when I asked him. I haven't heard from him since the final divorce decree.'' She gazed at him and spoke her deepest fear. ''I don't need to let another man with itchy feet into my life.''

It was more than that. Her concern for her children had to come before her growing attraction to Drew. If she gave in to the desire that filled her now, tonight, she might even begin to fall in love with another man just like Walt. She couldn't bring herself to even think about the heartbreak that might follow.

They had to get out of the shack before her resolve melted under the look of longing in Drew's eyes, a longing that echoed in her own heart.

Drew bit his lip and willed his body to cool. Maybe she was right. He'd led a nomadic life for so long he'd forgotten what it felt like to stay in one place. Not that he was going to apologize for the only life he'd known since he was a teenage boy. Still, recently he'd begun to sense somehow things had changed. He'd never felt alone before as he did now.

Wanting to have a woman like Leslie for his own was normal, he mused as he surveyed her green eyes, auburn hair and trim figure in the dim light. But, he was pragmatic enough to realize he didn't fit into her world, just as she didn't fit into the one he'd made for himself.

Maybe he could have taken advantage of Leslie's fears. But, with a woman like her, giving in to his growing desire would not only commit him to something he wasn't prepared for, it would hog-tie him hand and foot for the rest of his life.

Face it, he chided himself, the truth is the truth. Even if he and Leslie were compatible, and that was still in doubt, they had no future together. He wanted his freedom too much to throw it away. Even for a desirable woman like Leslie. She wanted stability, someone to make her world safe.

If he had any sense, he'd back off before it was too late.

"I'm sorry," he said at last, raking his fingers through his hair. "I guess I was out of line. But to be honest with you, it's been a long time for me too."

"Well, at least we know where we stand," she answered as she looked away. "Right now, the important thing is to find a way out of here."

"I've thought about everything that even seems remotely possible, but I'm afraid I'm stumped," he answered as he surveyed the room again. He reached for the note the kids had left behind, then sank into the lone rickety chair and read the message again. "So, where do we go from here? Do you have any ideas?"

Leslie shook her head. *Which is more important, the future or your attraction to this man?* her inner voice whispered.

In her turmoil, it would have been easy to accept the

comfort Drew had offered her. But there were choices to make, and she had to live with herself.

"Maybe we can do the 'get to know each other' part," Leslie answered at last. "At least we can be friends." She glanced at the cookies and apples. "I suppose we could start by sharing a meal together."

Drew managed to keep a straight face as he recalled the kid's handbills offering a reward for a man interested in matrimony, so they could have a dad. Friendship *definitely* hadn't been what the kids had had in mind.

What Leslie didn't know wouldn't hurt her, Drew thought grimly as he reached for an apple. But she was mighty naive if she really believed a friendship between them was all the boys had intended. Or, if she *was* trying to convince herself friendship was all they'd had in mind, it was okay for now. They had to somehow pass the time between now and when someone freed them.

At least she wasn't biting his head off for something that was beyond his control.

"What would you like to know about me?" Drew asked, taking a cookie. He was resigned to trading life stories instead of passing the time with something much more interesting.

"For starters, why did you come to Calico?" When Drew glanced sharply at her, she hurried on. "Sorry, I didn't mean it the way it sounded. I know you're a friend of Sheriff Carrey's, but of all places to wind up, Calico seems the least likely for a man like you."

"It's just another stop on the road," he answered with a shrug. He was tempted to tell her it hadn't mattered to him where he wound up, or what it was that drove him to keep on moving. He wasn't sure what had turned him into a rolling stone, anyway. Now that he was a grown man, he couldn't in good conscience blame his wanderlust on his aunt and uncle's impersonal treatment.

It was more than that. Looking for someone real or something meaningful had kept him moving on. He'd been called a maverick more than once. Maybe it was true.

"There's no mystery about me," Drew added. "It's just that I'm the restless type. I seem to feel the need to keep on moving."

"Why?"

Drew didn't like the cautious look she was giving him. And he was the guy who'd just assured her she didn't have to be frightened of him? "I don't have a police record and, in case you're interested, I'm not on the run from anyone. And not from the law, either, or Tom Carrey wouldn't have hired me," he added. "Now, if there's anything else you want to know about me, go ahead and ask. Otherwise, if we're going to play twenty questions, it's my turn."

"Sounds fair," Leslie answered as she glanced around for a place to sit. With a quick glance at him, she finally lowered herself to the edge of the narrow cot and nibbled at a cookie. "But you haven't really told me much. For instance, where did you come from and where are you going?"

"That one's easy," Drew replied, although leaving the only home he knew as a teenager hadn't been easy at all. He made himself as comfortable as possible in the small chair. "I was born in Temptation, Pennsylvania. Left when I was seventeen." He stretched his legs and eyed the cot with envy. "I've kept moving around, taking jobs here and there that interested me every month or two."

"Temptation? You made that one up!"

"Not at all. Temptation is a speck on the map, but it's a real little town, all right."

She didn't look as if she believed him for a minute. Not that he blamed her. There weren't many places with a name as tantalizing.

"Temptation doesn't make any more sense than the other little towns in Pennsylvania with whimsical names—Bird In Hand, Intercourse, Paradise," he went on. "I figure the folks who settled the farm country around Lancaster must have had a mistaken sense of humor. No, there wasn't a damned thing tempting about Temptation."

"So you intend to keep on moving?"

"I guess so." He shouldn't have been surprised at the look of disappointment that came into her eyes. Not after she'd told him what she thought about men who couldn't stay in one place for long. "At least until I find what I'm looking for," he amended.

She gazed back at him. The look on her face made him feel as if he was being measured and found wanting.

"It's my turn now," Drew said, anxious to get the conversation off him. "Since everyone around Calico seems to have come from someplace else, where are you from?"

"Barstow, just south of here. I was born and brought

up there. I stayed until I married and had the boys. After my divorce I came to Calico to open my shop. I became one of the few people who live here year-round when I decided it was a good place to raise the boys. From the way they've been acting lately, though, I'm not so sure.''

Drew nodded. ''After hearing Carrey touting Barstow, and Calico for that matter, I'd have to agree it seems as if this is as decent a place to raise children as any.''

''I suppose you're right.'' She managed a feeble smile. ''There isn't anything wrong with Barstow or Calico. Maybe the trouble is with Jeremy and Tim. Maybe they do need more attention than I've managed to give them.''

Drew couldn't resist voicing his thoughts. ''I'm sure you're doing all you can. But have you stopped to consider they're serious about wanting a dad?''

She bit her lip and kept the answer to herself.

As far as Drew could tell, Leslie was a nester, or she wouldn't have remained in one place all her life. A woman who needed a man with a nine-to-five job who would be home before dark. A man who would take an interest in his wife and children.

''Where did you meet Tom Carrey?''

Drew pulled his mind back to their game of twenty questions.

''When I tied up with a rodeo a couple of years back. He was passing through on business and mentioned Calico. Told me to look him up when I was ready to settle down.''

''And are you?''

"Ready to settle down in Calico? No, I don't think so," Drew answered. Not when the lady in front of him was preparing to set down laws and rules for him and everyone else in Calico to live by. Rules made him nervous.

A silence fell between them.

"Then you're moving on?" she said finally. When he didn't answer, she added, "Even a man with itchy feet has to settle down somewhere."

"Maybe. I've agreed to stay at least a week," he answered evasively. "I tend to take things one at a time. Right now, I'd say I don't really have a choice."

Suddenly, a crash of thunder sounded. Jagged streaks of lightning flashed outside the small window. A gust of wind found its way through the cracks in the door and rattled the table. The flashlight fell to the floor.

"It's a hell of a time for a summer storm," Drew muttered. He scrambled for the flashlight and checked to see if it still worked. "I don't even know how long these batteries will last. But..." He saw Leslie shivering uncontrollably. "Hold on a minute." He sat down beside her and wrapped the blanket around her shoulders. "This ought to keep you warm enough."

"Thank you." She sighed. "I guess we'll be all right, but I'm not sure how I feel about the boys— angry or worried. What if they're out in the desert in this storm?"

"I'm sure they're okay," Drew assured her. "The note said they were going home to bed. A storm like this is likely to keep them there. Besides, they have each other for company. You have nothing to worry about." Thunder rolled outside. The weathered shack seemed to tremble on its foundation. Leslie moved closer to him.

Another blast of thunder rocked the shack, followed hard on its heels by a flash of lightning that lit up the room. Leslie moaned under her breath and seemed to shrink into the thin blanket.

"Still cold?"

"Yes. And maybe a little frightened, too," she answered honestly. "Although I hate to admit it. Storms have always gotten to me," she added with a shudder. "It's a good thing the boys aren't here to see me make a coward of myself."

Drew knew by now how much Leslie prided herself on her control of herself and her surroundings. It had to be more than the summer storm that was affecting her.

Extraordinary circumstances called for heroic measures.

Drew put his arm around her and pulled her close to his chest. "Here, let me keep you warm." She turned her face into his shoulder with a drawn-out sigh. He knew it was tempting fate to have her in his arms again, but if ever anyone needed to be held and comforted, it was Leslie.

Her soft, warm breath against his neck sent Drew's thoughts careering back to the passionate kiss of a few minutes ago. He murmured words of comfort into her silken hair even as his thoughts turned to something more intimate.

"How long did you say it's been since a man held you?" he asked softly.

"I don't think about it much anymore, but it seems

like forever," Leslie replied, her voice muffled against his chest.

Drew caressed her cheek lightly as he considered the problem confronting him. He could take her mind off the storm by giving in to the passion he felt. Or he could just hold her in his arms until they got through the night. There were choices to make and the answer was clear.

It couldn't be easy for Leslie, a single mother with two children to raise by herself. She didn't need any more trouble than she already had. Struck again by her determination to make a new life for herself and her kids, Drew settled for holding her.

When she shivered once more, he lowered her to the bed and stretched out beside her. She started to protest, but he hushed her with a gentle finger on her lips. "For whatever time we'll be locked up in here, I'll keep you warm—nothing else."

"Nothing else?" she echoed, the doubt in her voice clear.

"Nothing else, I promise," he assured her. "Now, try and go to sleep."

"Feel warmer?" he asked after she finally relaxed in his arms.

She nodded, a small sigh escaping her lips. "Maybe a little."

Drew tucked the blanket more closely around her shoulders and gently stroked her hair. It took all his strength not to lift her face to his and lose himself in her lips. "Better?" he asked.

"Much better," she answered sleepily. "But how about you? You must be pretty cold and tired yourself by now. It's been a rough day and desert nights can be awfully cold.''

Cold? Drew couldn't tell her that he was practically burning up with wanting her. That he could feel every beat of his heart as it pulsated in his chest. That he wanted her more and more with every breath he took.

He thought of being immersed in ice-cold water. Of tramping through waist-high snow back in Temptation. Of all the reasons why he couldn't do anything more than hold her. Of all the reasons why he had to remember that the road ahead of him, while unknown, was long. And that he intended to start down it when the week he'd agreed to was over. No image helped— he wanted her more than ever.

"I'm fine," he lied. "There's enough heat coming off the blanket to keep me warm.'' *And from her warm breath, her heated rosy skin as she nestled closer.*

"I'm willing to share," she whispered.

"Don't even think about it," he answered. "Just try to go to sleep. Morning isn't that far away."

In seconds, her even breathing told him she'd taken him at his word and had fallen asleep.

If things had been different between them, he would have taken the chance to show her how much he wanted her. He would have made her his and, maybe, even filled both their empty hearts—if only for the few remaining days and nights he would be here. Given the opportunity, he would have left them both with happy memories.

She was everything he'd dreamed of when he was young and still believed in happy-ever-after. Before his world had stopped still and he'd given up believing in fairy tales with happy endings.

He knew he had no business spending the night comforting Leslie instead of trying to find a way out of the shack while she slept. But she felt too good to put out of his arms.

He'd wait until there was more light, he told himself. In the meantime, he couldn't bring himself to draw away. He rested his face against her sweet-smelling hair and closed his eyes.

Who was he kidding? Drew thought as he let sleep overtake him. All his thoughts involving Leslie were pipe dreams. The kiss they'd shared had been an impulse. The only reason she was letting him hold her in his arms now was that she was worried, cold and more than a little frightened.

She'd already made it clear she didn't trust men like him.

Chapter Five

The screeching sound of wood and nails giving way gradually penetrated Drew's subconscious. It was followed by two young voices and the deep, gravelly voice of an older man.

Young voices? Older man?

For a moment, Drew couldn't remember where he was or what he was doing here. He struggled to open his eyes.

"Don't that beat all!" the deep voice muttered.

"Cool," one young voice chimed in.

"Yeah, real cool," the other young voice echoed.

Drew awakened slowly as the voices sank in. It took him a full moment to focus on his surroundings. Sure enough, the weathered wooden walls, the dirt floor and the few pieces of rickety furniture were still there—just as they'd been last night. The abandoned miner's shack in all its pitiful glory hadn't been a bad dream, after all. It was real—dirt, cobwebs and all. And just as real was the sleeping figure of Leslie Chambers curled up on the cot beside him.

Sometime during the night, she'd turned her back and nestled into the warmth of his body. They'd wound up cuddled like a couple of spoons with his arms holding her close to him.

Before he had a chance to enjoy her softness, the clean, sweet smell of her, the realization they had an audience jarred him wide-awake.

Chagrined that he and Leslie had been caught in what seemed like a compromising position, he looked over his shoulder to stare at the unwelcome intruders. Three pairs of eyes were regarding him with unfeigned interest.

It was a hell of a time to be rescued.

He held his breath, glanced down at Leslie to make sure she was still asleep, and wondered what he'd done to deserve the mess he'd found himself in.

Drew cursed under his breath and paused long enough to cover Leslie with the small blanket before he slowly disengaged himself. He rolled to his feet, loosened his belt, unbuckled his jeans and tucked in the shirt that had managed to free itself during the night. Heaving a sigh at the obvious implications of his loose shirt, he confronted the trio by the door: a spellbound Jeremy and Tim, and to make matters worse, Alan Little, the livery stable owner. Since Leslie had not awakened, Drew motioned for them to be quiet and ushered them outside.

The kids looked fit and safe, and for some reason, pleased with themselves. He fixed them with a cold stare—he figured he'd set them straight on *that* in a hurry.

The burly livery owner, who held a crowbar in one hand, looked as though he'd just won the lottery. The only one present who was unhappy with the situation was Drew.

"What are you doing here, Alan?" Drew asked. Through narrowed eyes, he sent a threatening look at the man's small companions.

"We couldn't get the door open when we came back to let you out," Jeremy answered. "So we asked Mr. Little to come and help."

"I was speaking to Mr. Little," Drew said dryly. "Your turn will come later."

Drew felt mighty stupid just thinking about what he and Leslie must have looked like lying together on the narrow cot. Not to mention his partial state of undress. Even though he'd behaved like a saint last night, he knew he still looked—and felt—guilty as hell.

Maybe because his thoughts had been far from innocent.

It was a good thing he had a sense of humor or he would have been mortified at being caught like this. He hoped Leslie would see the funny side of it all when she awakened.

"I was barely out of bed and fixing to go over to Maddie's for breakfast when the kids charged into the livery stable this morning," the livery owner explained. "They said it was an emergency and asked me to come help get you out of this shack. I locked up and brought them out here right away." He grinned knowingly at Drew, then winked. "I don't think you need my help, though. Looks like you were doing well enough on your own."

At the mention of breakfast, Drew's salivary glands had involuntarily reacted. But when the meaning of the man's sly comment about Leslie and Drew "not need-ing any help" registered, his temper flared. If they'd been alone, he would have punched the guy out for the wisecrack, but the kids were watching. "What in the hell do you mean by that?"

The livery stable owner took a step backward at the menacing tone in Drew's voice. "Nothing, nothing at all," he stammered. "Just funnin'."

Hardly mollified, but not willing to press the issue with a young audience, Drew nodded. He'd have a talk with the man later and make sure he didn't start any rumors. "Did the boys bring your horses back?"

"Yeah, last night. In fact, they apologized for taking them without my permission. They even paid me twenty dollars for the loan of the horses. And they've promised you would give me another ten for getting you out of here."

"They did, did they?" Drew exchanged knowing glances with Jeremy and Tim. He knew they were broke as well as they did.

They might look like two innocent little angels this morning, but they sure as hell had behaved like two devils last night. The thought struck him that if they'd been willing to spend the reward money they'd offered for the man who would marry their mother for the "loan" of the two horses, they must have been pretty damn sure their investment would be worthwhile.

As for him paying the man ten dollars to use a crow-bar to open the door to the shack this morning, he might have been willing to ante up last night just to get out of here. But this morning? He'd take the money out of the kids' hides before he paid out a penny of his own money

"You going to press charges against these two horse thieves?" Drew inquired with a quelling glance at the boys. He figured the look alone ought to give the kids something to think about for a while. Or at least, that it was enough to remind them he still had a score to settle with them.

"Nah," Little replied, looking relieved now that the heat was off himself and onto the kids. "Twenty dollars for the afternoon ain't bad, considering business ain't all that great."

From the look of things, the kids had obviously thought twenty dollars wasn't too much to gain a dad, either.

"Say, how did you two manage to get yourselves locked in here in the first place?" Little inquired, arching his neck to peer into the shack over Drew's shoulder as sounds from within indicated that Leslie was beginning to stir.

"It's a long story," Drew answered cautiously, grateful that Leslie had been too exhausted by last night's misadventure to awaken earlier. He stepped in front of the doorway to block Little's view. "And I'm sure you don't want to hear it."

"Oh, I don't know about that," the man replied with a broad grin. "Me and some of the rest of the folks I know would be mighty interested."

Leslie's voice came from inside the shack. "Drew? Is someone out there with you? Did you manage to get the door open?"

"No, but you might say your children did," Drew answered. "With a little help."

Leslie appeared and, for a moment, froze at the tableau in front of her. Then she rushed to hug the children and gather them in her arms. "Are you all right?" she cried as she ran her hands over their hair, their faces, their shoulders as if to assure herself they were in one piece.

"'Morning, Ms. Chambers." Little took off his hat and grinned broadly. "Sure glad to see you're okay. We missed you last night. Folks were kind of worried when you didn't show up for the meeting."

The town hall meeting!

Leslie's relief turned to anger. She'd not only missed her first major test as the mayor of Calico, she would probably be the topic of gossip for days and weeks to come. Judging from the look on Alan Little's face, it was clear Calico would soon know she'd spent the night in their deputy sheriff's arms.

She turned on the boys. "How could you have locked me in here? What in heaven's name were you thinking of? And after I told you I'd called for a town hall meeting last night?"

"Gosh, Mom," Jeremy replied. "We forgot there was going to be a meeting. We thought you'd be pleased at spending the night with Mr. McClain."

"Pleased? Pleased at what?" she retorted, blinking to banish the sleep from her eyes. "For making a fool out of me?"

Tim spoke up for the first time in his own defense. "No, honest, Mom. We just thought you ought to get to know Mr. McClain. He's really cool. Jeremy and I like him a lot.''

Drew winced. Cool? After he'd read them the riot act, made them apologize for the dynamite caper and then set them to sweeping Calico's boardwalks? Or after he'd narrowly rescued them from their handbill campaign for a dad?

He'd never seen such a single-minded couple of kids in his life, nor minds that worked overtime with such drastic results. As for finding a dad, they were going after their prey like a hungry lion hunting for his next meal. Too bad it was beginning to look as if he was their target.

He squinted thoughtfully at the boys and shook his head. Maybe they'd mistaken his attempts to keep them out of trouble for interest in their hunt for a dad. Whatever the reason, the kids had taken to him faster than ducks take to water.

Between the two, the kids had managed to create enough trouble to keep a small army of deputies busy.

''Anyway, Mom, maybe now you can *both* win the bet!'' Tim added eagerly.

''Bet? What bet?'' Leslie demanded sharply.

Tim sent Drew a pleading glance.

Alan Little cleared his throat as if he was about to speak.

Drew jumped into the fray before the man could open his mouth. The last thing Drew needed was to have Leslie find out what he and Tim had overheard in the Silver Dollar saloon about the bet.

''Forget it, Alan,'' he warned before he answered Leslie. ''It's not worth talking about. Actually, there's been some kind of mistake.'' Drew eyed the trio with a warning look that should have sent them running for cover.

The boys managed to act properly cowed. The smirk on Alan Little's face gave him away. In spite of Drew's warning, it was pretty clear the man would broadcast the story all over town as soon as he got back. Not that Drew knew the details behind the bet, but he'd begun to put together the pieces of the conversation he'd overheard. The answer fried him.

Betting on him taming Leslie Chambers? Fat chance. Any man around who was still willing to try was asking for trouble, and it sure wasn't going to be him. Even if Leslie had somehow managed to worm her way under his skin.

It was a good thing he had a sense of humor.

Something told him the other subject of the bet didn't.

Until he found out more about what the men had been discussing in the saloon, he fervently hoped Leslie would remain in the dark. With her temper, they'd all be lucky if they wound up in one piece once she heard about it.

One thing was certain. As soon as he had a chance, he intended to bump a few heads together for getting him involved in what looked to be a hopeless case.

Little cleared his throat and smiled broadly. ''Excuse me, folks. I think I'd better leave now and get the livery open. You want me to take the kids back to town?''

Comical or not, Drew felt the situation was on the verge of getting out of hand. Speaking of hand, his still itched to punch the smile off the man's face.

"No," Drew answered firmly. "They're coming back with me. I'll catch up with you later."

Little nodded, put his hat back on his head and left, with a last speculative look at Leslie.

Drew waited until the man was out of earshot before he confronted a wide-eyed Jeremy and Tim. "The two of you are going back with me," he said firmly. "We have a few things to clear up. Go on inside the shack and wait for me while I talk to your mother. I'll call you in a minute."

Leslie watched the door close behind the boys before she set into him.

"Wait a minute! I'm not any happier about this than you are. But whatever you have to discuss with the boys can wait until I get them home. This isn't the time or the place."

"As far as I'm concerned, it is," Drew replied. His frustration boiled over. "I'm through being Mr. Nice Guy! This is between me and the boys. I said I'd take care of this and I will. You go on home and wait for them."

"Not without the boys, I'm not," Leslie snapped. "As far as I can see, if you'd been keeping a closer eye on them, this would never have happened!"

As soon as the words were out of her mouth, Leslie bit her lip. She was torn between anger at what her children had done and relief that they were okay. That, and feeling mortified at having been discovered with Drew.

After a night spent innocently in his arms, she knew she owed Drew the opposite of anger. She was worldly enough to know that most other men would have taken advantage of her fear of last night's storm.

She remembered being tempted by his raw masculinity and the sheer pleasure of being held in his arms. How she'd been tempted to return his kisses, and to ask for more. How she'd ached to ease the longing that had come over her when he'd held her and kissed her and turned her orderly world upside down.

She hadn't given in to her awakened desires because she'd been afraid of making the same mistake she'd made with Walt—falling in love with the wrong man again. If she and Drew had made love last night, it might have been the start of something she wasn't prepared to finish. And from what he'd told her last night, neither was he.

She'd been afraid to tempt fate. To find out where a relationship with him might have taken her.

To add to her guilt, she'd been aware Drew had been as aroused as she had been. Even so, he'd been decent and honorable—a man of his word. In an uncomfortable situation, he'd been a comfortable man to be with. And, if she were truthful with herself, she had to admit he was innocent of initiating their kidnapping.

As she stared at Drew, she realized with a shock that while her anger had been directed at him, she'd actually been frustrated with herself for wanting him.

Drew deserved more from her than harsh words. But now that the words had been said, she knew no apology could take them back.

Drew stared at her in shock. After all the trouble he'd been through trying to keep the boys in line, not to mention trying to fulfill his limited duties as deputy sheriff, she was blaming him for their getting kidnapped last night?

"Are you saying this was all my fault?" he demanded.

"Some of it, yes," Leslie amended, with an uneasy glance at him. "I just meant that if you'd kept a closer watch on those two while they were supposed to be with you, they wouldn't have had a chance to take the horses, let alone have time to plan to lock us up in here."

Drew threw her a disgusted look, gave up and thrust his hat back on his head. This tirade was from a woman who had bared her soul to him and then spent the night in his arms? The least he had expected was a simple expression of gratitude. Especially since he hadn't taken advantage of her even though he'd ached to show her he was there for her with more than words. Instead, all he'd gotten for his nobility was a large dose of undeserved blame.

Even a thank-you would have been nice.

Hell, he thought as he shrugged and turned to leave, he should have known this was how the misadventure was going to turn out. He hadn't gotten many kind words from Leslie Chambers before now—just what had he expected would change even after a night spent together in each other's arms? As for her attempts to make him feel guilty, as far as he was concerned, he didn't have a damn thing to feel guilty about.

"Okay, if that's the way you want it," he answered, and striding to the cabin door, opened it and said, "Tim and Jeremy, come on out." Turning to Leslie, he continued, "I'll leave the boys to you from now on. Seems to me, if you haven't been able to straighten them out in all this time, you're not going to be able to do much about them now. But be my guest. I'm out of here, starting now.''

He got into his van and slammed the door.

Tim and Jeremy, coming out the shack, started to move toward the Land Rover. He shook his head and waved them off through the open window. ''Go on home with your mother,'' he said, hardening his heart at the apprehensive looks they cast at Leslie.

Too bad things had turned out this way, Drew thought as he drove through the painted hills back to Calico. But the last thing he should have been thinking of was that he could be friends with Leslie Chambers. Or, even more than just friends.

She'd made it pretty clear from the first that she had no use for men like him, or men in general, for that matter. Not that he blamed her, in his case. She didn't know much about him. On the other hand, he thought bitterly, she hadn't given herself a chance to know him, either. But he knew one thing by now. Even if she didn't care for him, she seemed to like his kisses well enough.

Damn it all, he thought as he tromped on the gas pedal and shot down the hill in a cloud of dust, in spite of the way she'd reacted to the kidnapping, he found himself still taken with her.

He thrust the thought away and blamed it on his blasted testosterone. Thinking of Leslie as a desirable woman was a no-win situation. He'd take one day at a time until his commitment to Tom Carrey was finished and he'd move on. But there was something he had to take care of first before Leslie got wind of it.

The bet. And the men who had made it.

WHEN DREW PULLED UP to his quarters behind the jail-house, he noticed Keith Andrews hurrying up the boardwalk from the livery stable to the saloon. Andrews wasn't the only man headed in that direction, for that matter. Identifiable by their period regalia, at least three other Calico residents were entering the swinging door. Little couldn't have beaten him back by more than thirty minutes, but it looked as if the news he'd brought back with him was spreading like wildfire.

"Hold up there a minute, Andrews," he called. "I want to talk to you."

"Can it wait?" Andrews replied as he barely slowed his stride to let Drew catch up with him. "I'm in a hurry."

"You don't say?" Drew remarked as he joined the tintype photographer. "What's up?"

"Well, if you must know," Andrews said impatiently, "I'm on my way to a meeting."

"A meeting?"

"Don't act so innocent, McClain," Andrews said sarcastically, "you know as well as I do that there's a betting pool going on. And from what I just heard it's payout time!"

"Maybe not." Drew stepped in front of Andrews and halted him in his tracks. "It happens that I *don't* know as much about the bet as I'd like to. Why don't you explain it to me so we'll both know what's going on?"

"Hell," Andrews remarked as he glanced longingly at the swinging door to the saloon. "Maybe you don't know all the details, but it sure concerns you and Leslie Chambers in the shack last night."

"Nothing happened last night," Drew remarked. "As for the bet, I'm sure as hell going to know all about it in the next two minutes or..." He left the threat unfinished.

"Well, I guess it won't make a difference if I spell it out for you," Andrews answered. "I can get my share of the winnings anytime."

"Keep on talking." Drew's lips tightened.

"After the way you and our mayor went at it the other day at Maddie's, Frank and Herb decided to get a pool going on who was going to come out ahead. A bunch of us bet that you could tame our mayor, one way or another, and make her like it," Andrews blurted. He backed off when he saw the anger flare in Drew's eyes. "Hey, it wasn't my idea! I just took advantage of the betting. I wanted to win the bet myself!"

"That's about the most stupid idea I ever heard," Drew retorted. "Just who did you guys get to bet against you?"

"Maddie Hanks and a parcel of fool women she lined up, that's who." Andrews smirked as he returned Drew's cold stare. "They bet us that our mayor is too smart to let you get the best of her."

Drew eyed the antsy photographer. "You lose," he said. "It looks as if you guys jumped the gun. As far as I'm concerned, Ms. Chambers is still fancy-free and likely to stay that way. She didn't have any more to do with me last night than she does with the rest of you upstanding male citizens of Calico."

"Hey, wait a minute. Are you sure anybody'll believe that? When Alan found the both of you in bed, and you partially dressed, he as good as confirmed you came out ahead."

Drew bit his tongue. He couldn't take back last night but he hated the thought that he might have unintentionally had a hand in making mud out of Leslie's reputation. She might be a spitfire, but she deserved the town's respect. After all, she'd volunteered to be their mayor at a job that probably paid one dollar a year, if anything. He thought rapidly. Maybe if he was clear that he didn't plan on staying in Calico, they'd let up on her.

"Not that it's any of your damned business, but I guarantee to you that nothing happened last night, and that I'm going to be moving on soon," Drew replied. "Now, if I were you, I'd forget all about the bet. There's nothing to bet on. Do your friends a favor and pass the word along."

"Well, I guess that leaves the field wide open, doesn't it?" Andrews grinned his satisfaction.

"Wide open for what?" Something about the grin told Drew the situation was about to go to hell. For sure, it wasn't comical any longer. Not that he ever thought it was, in spite of Little's comments at the cabin.

"For me to go courting," Andrews replied, preening as he spoke. "Our mayor is all woman behind that cold shell of hers, even if she does pretend she's not inter-

ested in getting married again. I know just how to butter her up and to persuade her to reconsider.''

"Good luck. You're going to need it, with Leslie,''
Drew answered mildly, seething inside at the thought
of Keith Andrews getting close to Leslie. He was surprised to find himself jealous! Jealous? How could he
be jealous when he wasn't even sure he *liked* the lady?
Her kisses, yes, but that was something else.

"Leslie?'' Andrews echoed. "How come you're on
first-name terms? I thought you said she didn't want
anything to do with you.'' He laughed gleefully.
"Maybe Alan was right about last night, after all.
Looks like I can collect both ways.''

Drew balled his fists. "Just what do you mean by
that?''

Andrews preened again and straightened his celluloid collar and tie. "Our mayor doesn't know it yet,
but she's going to be the next Mrs. Andrews. I'll get
the reward and my share of the bet, too. In fact, I'm
pretty sure the relationship will wind up to be pure
profit for me. As for the kids, I know just how to handle
those two juvenile delinquents. They'll settle down fast
enough when I whip them into shape.''

Drew shuddered. "Look, I'm not going to tell you
again. The lady isn't free for the taking. That goes for
the kids, too!''

"Hell, what do you know about it?'' Andrews answered. "Your job is to keep the peace and enforce
the law. Marrying Leslie Chambers ain't illegal!'' He
whipped around and disappeared into the saloon.

Drew strode back to the jail, his determination growing by the minute. He might not be planning to remain

in Calico much longer, but he intended to keep an eye on Leslie while he was here—and the kids, too, for that matter.

If for no other reason than to see Leslie take that supercilious smile off of Andrew's face and that swagger out of his walk.

Chapter Six

His arms loaded with split wood railings, Drew headed up the street to start the repair of the back porch of Leslie's shop. A carpenter's belt filled with small tools, miscellaneous nails and hardware hung loosely around his waist. He'd carried it with him during his travels, picking up odd carpentry jobs here and there when the opportunity offered.

He inhaled the fresh morning air as he strode. Cumulus clouds, nudged along gently by a mild summer breeze, floated across a blue sky above him. In the distance, the softly colored hills against which Calico nestled resembled one of Leslie's patchwork quilts. It was a warm and comforting thought.

He nodded amiably when greeted. The lack of activity around the saloon told him Andrews had spread the word about Drew's comments. Hopefully, the bet had been called off. For now, everything seemed right with the world.

He'd decided this morning was as good a time as any to put the kids to work replacing the railing of the shop's back porch. It would also give him a covert excuse to keep an eye on Leslie. If Andrews saw him around the shop often enough in the next few days, maybe the guy would get the message that Leslie was off limits.

He'd told himself he was actually going through with the repair job for the sake of Jeremy and Tim. In spite of what he'd told Leslie about being quit of the boys, he couldn't bring himself to turn his back on them or to treat them the distant way he'd been treated as a youngster. The kids needed to know someone besides their mother cared about them.

Actually, although it continued to surprise him, it was beginning to look as if he'd fallen like a ton of bricks for Leslie—red hair, temper and all.

He smiled ruefully when he recalled how they'd shared the single, narrow and uncomfortable cot last night. And how he'd enjoyed having her in his arms in spite of his frustration at having to cool his growing desire for her. The kiss they'd shared earlier hadn't lasted long enough for him. The silken pressure of her soft cheek against his remained a fond memory. And so was the memory of the even rise and fall of her breasts against his arms as she slept.

In another time or place, he would have made love to her until they'd satisfied the hunger he'd instinctively sensed was the same for both of them.

He hadn't felt that close to anyone for more years than he could remember, he reflected, as he turned into the alley and to the back door of the Quilt Lady. Last night had been the first time since he'd lost his parents that he could actually remember feeling a connection to another person. Or even a glimmer of a need for someone to call his own.

Until last night, he'd almost believed he wasn't capable of actually caring for anyone, or having someone care for him. But he'd wanted Leslie then, and he wanted her now.

Even her put-down, after she'd realized the boys were safe, hadn't made him stop wanting her. Not after he'd had a chance to realize she'd behaved like an anxious mother before she could allow herself to behave like a woman.

Tame her? Hell, no. In spite of feeling frustrated more times than he cared to admit, he liked her just as she was. Not that he was willing to risk another put-down by telling her so.

And no way was anyone going to use her or abuse her if he had anything to say about it.

He set the stack of railings on the back porch and quietly entered the shop. The object of his interest was cutting pieces of fabric and setting them in neat piles. She wore his favorite shade of green: the color of the rolling farmlands around Temptation. Her auburn hair had been braided and framed her lovely face. Before today, he hadn't noticed the tiny sprinkle of freckles over her cheeks that made her younger, softer.

He even liked the way she bit her lower lip in concentration while she measured and cut away, humming to herself under her breath.

In her quaint costume, she was the perfect picture of nineteenth-century femininity. She actually resembled an old-fashioned woman out of a painting he'd seen in some museum during his travels. Since he was secretly an old-fashioned kind of guy himself, he took a few minutes to enjoy the view.

A pleasing aroma permeated the shop. The woodsy apple scent reminded him of the stand of fruit trees behind his boyhood home on a small farm in Temptation. A feeling of nostalgia for the carefree days of his early years and the loving parents he'd known hit him square in the gut.

Maybe it was those early times he'd been trying to recapture during his wandering, he reflected idly as he watched Leslie. He'd moved restlessly from place to place, hoping to recognize the right moment, the right place and the right person when he came across them. He'd come up empty time after time. Until today.

When a frown came over her face, he wondered what Leslie was thinking of. Last night?

He cleared his throat.

Leslie glanced up and felt herself blush at Drew's close scrutiny.

He was tall and lithe, strong and masculine, and had walked in right out of her thoughts. His dark eyes shone as his lips curved in a lopsided smile. His hair, ruffled by the morning breeze, curled against his forehead. She had to resist the temptation to reach out and touch him, to see if he was truly real or merely the result of wishful thinking.

With him came the memories of last night, of being held in his arms, pressed against his solid body. A night spent longing for a dream just out of her reach. She'd been stirred by his warmth, his firm strength. Had even been tempted to give in to the desire that filled her. Because she hadn't been able to face him with those thoughts playing in her mind, she remembered turning

over to face the tar-papered wall of the shack instead
of his all-seeing eyes.

Afraid she might have been given away by a sigh
that escaped her, she'd forced herself to breathe evenly
as though she was asleep. A sleep that had escaped her
until early morning.

"Why, hello!" she managed. "After last night, I
thought you'd have been gone by now."

"No," he answered with that suggestive grin of his.
"I told you I'd see the week through and I'm a man
of my word." He sauntered over, all innocent charm.

He didn't fool her for a minute. She'd been around
her boys long enough to know he was up to something.
She was about to ask, but, to her chagrin, his freshly
shampooed cinnamon-colored hair was only inches
away from her nose. The pleasing scent of his shaving
lotion filled her senses. Even the tiny cut on his chin
intrigued her.

Fleetingly, she wondered what it would have been
like if she'd given in to the desire that had swept over
her. Given in to the magnetic look in his eyes. But
she'd realized then, as she realized now, that physical
attraction wasn't enough. She wanted more.

"I promised I would show the boys how to repair
the back porch railing, and here I am," he commented.
"I didn't know if you had any tools, so I brought my
own."

Leslie tore her gaze from his full lips and glanced at
the carpenter's belt loaded with small tools that hung
around his waist. He might have come on legitimate
business, but she was in no hurry to find out. She was
too busy recalling how he'd looked early the other

morning when he'd come striding up the street with Maddie.

Involuntarily, she pictured him as he'd been then, with his chest bare, his skin glistening after a shower. His broad shoulders sporting a towel that hadn't covered near enough of him. And, of all things, the way his jeans had hung loosely around his lean hips!

Everything about Drew McClain told her he was a dangerous man. Dangerous to her carefully ordered life, to the hard shell she'd built around her to protect herself. And to her hard-won peace of mind. How could she want this man, when he was the last man she should want?

But fair was fair. She had some apologies to make.

"About last night…" She got no further when he quirked an eyebrow. The smile that curved at his lips grew more inviting.

"What about last night?" His eyes sparkled with an invitation as he waited for her answer.

It was too much. How could she keep her mind on the apology she owed him when the suggestion in his voice and the look in his eyes spoke of things better left unsaid.

"Behave yourself," she admonished, even as she smothered an answering smile. "You're no better than the other men around here, always trying to get my goat. I only intended to apologize for the boys' behavior yesterday."

She hesitated, took a deep breath and plunged ahead while she still had her wits about her.

"I also need to apologize for my own behavior. I'm afraid I said things I should never have said. What I

should have done was to thank you for being there for
me and the boys, instead of blaming you for something
that wasn't your fault.''

''No need to apologize.'' Drew gazed down at Leslie
with a puzzled smile. She was like the small desert
chameleons that inhabited Calico. Changeable, even as
he watched them scuttle across the floor of the jailhouse. She could be furious with him one moment and
soft and appealing the next. At the moment, she looked
so sweet and feminine he couldn't understand how
she'd gotten her reputation as the Ice Lady. And how
she'd managed to keep the entire male population of
Calico at bay.

One thing was clear. At the rate things were going,
he'd never be able to keep one step ahead of her or to
understand his reaction to her.

Leslie *was* all woman and damned attractive. She
had too much to offer a lucky man to remain single
much longer. In one respect, Keith Andrews had been
right. It was only a matter of time before the right man
came along. But he'd be damned if it was going to be
Andrews.

Young as they were, her boys must have sensed it,
too. Rather than gamble on fate, they'd decided to take
matters into their own hands. Maybe it was more than
a dad for themselves that the boys were looking for—
maybe they were looking for a husband for their
mother. Whatever the reason, he had a growing feeling
things were coming to a head.

''I'm sure the boys meant well,'' he replied. ''As for
what you threw at me last night, I'm sure you were too
upset to think straight.''

"I'm afraid so," Leslie agreed. Looking uncomfortable, she dropped her eyes to the scissors in her hand, then lifted them again to gaze steadily at him. "But still, that was no excuse for what I said."

"Consider it forgotten," Drew assured her as he reluctantly put aside more intimate thoughts than her apology.

When her lips curved in a grateful smile, Drew couldn't help but think back to when he'd held her in his arms throughout a too-short night. He stirred uneasily.

"Now, as I was saying," he forged ahead, turning away to hide his reaction to her appealing smile. "I came to get the boys started on repairing the porch railings."

"You really don't need to do that," Leslie answered as she returned her attention to arranging the squares of material on the work table beside her. "I'm sure I can hire a handyman as soon as—"

"You don't need a handyman for what I have in mind," Drew cut in. "Not as long as you have me."

Leslie felt herself flush at his remark. *As long as she had him?* Unbidden thoughts rushed through her. "And just what *do* you have in mind?"

"Certainly not what you're thinking," Drew answered with a lazy grin. "I was only referring to the porch out back."

"Oh!" Leslie felt herself on fire again. Just what was there about the man that made her insides dissolve like a bowl of melted ice cream? She tried to force her thoughts back to the subject at hand. What had they been talking about? Porch railings? Yes, that was it.

She couldn't bring herself to tell him she had to hold off on the repairs until she'd sold another quilt or two in her stock. That the little extra money she was able to earn during the town's special events was needed for more important things.

The boys were growing by leaps and bounds, she thought worriedly. They seemed to outgrow their clothing faster than she was able to supply replacements. Thank goodness Tim was able to fit into some of the things Jeremy could no longer wear.

But she couldn't tell any of this to Drew, the one man she'd found herself attracted to since her divorce. She had to keep reminding herself he was a wandering man—another man who would only bring her pain and leave her with empty arms when he waved goodbye.

"Where are the boys?" Drew asked. "I figured you'd be keeping a tight rein on them nowadays." He turned to wander around the shop to give them both breathing space. "Looks as if you could use a few repairs around here, too."

"Yes, well, they'll have to wait until another time, too," Leslie answered. Along with the dozen other small repair jobs that were on her "someday" list. "The boys are out somewhere delivering handbills."

"Handbills?" Drew swung around and felt himself blanch. "What kind of handbills would that be?" he asked cautiously.

She gazed at him in surprise. "The chamber of commerce of Barstow hired them to distribute handbills at the entrance to Calico, touting Hullabaloo Days."

"The chamber of commerce hired them? You mean for real money?"

"Yes. A penny a handbill." She had to smile at the relieved expression on his face. "It may not be a lot of money, but it'll help."

"To do what?"

"To pay Alan Little the ten dollars they promised him if he let us out of the shack this morning. It seems they got the message you didn't intend to bail them out of their promise."

Drew relaxed as she explained. The handbills the kids were distributing had to be a whole different ball game than the ones he'd destroyed. His pulse had started to beat normally again—until he got a good look at Leslie.

He was drawn to the becoming blush that came over her face when their eyes met. So she hadn't forgotten the night they'd spent together, or the kiss and the hours she'd spent in his arms either. If she'd been half as aware of his clamoring desire as he'd been aware of her sensuality, no wonder she was turning a becoming shade of pink.

"I wish I could say the boys didn't have to pay Alan, since one of the horses was theirs and they'd already given him twenty dollars," he said, "but I figure making them pay up is the only way they'll stop to think the next time they come up with a fool idea."

Drew eyed Leslie as he spoke. She'd taken off her shoes and bare toes embellished with pink nail polish peeked from under her dress. Other than that, she was covered from the lace trim of the neckline of her dress to her ankles. No jeans today, he thought with mild regret. But maybe that was just as well. Maybe he would be able to keep his mind on his reason for coming here and not on the trim and inviting figure he kept envisioning under the dress.

Leslie looked down at the stack of material she was trying to match. Avoiding Drew's gaze was the only way she knew how to hide the way he affected her. She couldn't afford to give herself away. Drew McClain was the last man she wanted to encourage.

"The boys are also passing out a notice that I've called another town hall meeting for tonight," she added. "I hope you're planning to attend."

"Guess we'll have to stay away from miners' shacks if we plan on going through with the meeting," he joked.

His innocent comment wasn't so innocent at that, she thought as she glanced up at him. Not when his dark eyes were sparkling with something that made her middle tingle.

She forced her thoughts away from the reason she'd missed the last meeting. "With Hullabaloo Days just around the corner, we have to set up some procedures," she said firmly. "The town's been playing it by ear up until now. It's time we had some ground rules in place."

Caught with his mind on more intimate subjects, especially after the mention of the missed meeting, Drew managed to get the gist of what Leslie was planning to do: turn Calico into another highly structured town with enough rules and regulations to strangle a man. What would happen then to Calico's charm as a nineteenth-century mining town?

"Ground rules? Sounds as if you folks have been

doing okay without them until now. Aren't you a little late?"

"No," she answered firmly. "It's just that we've all been so wound up in our own affairs, we've forgotten how fast Calico is growing. Hullabaloo is just around the corner, and it usually brings in hundreds of extra tourists. But it's not only the celebration," she continued earnestly. "We need to have some kind of written rules to live by." She eyed him meaningfully. "As the law around here, you ought to appreciate that."

Drew's blood cooled at her words. *Rules to live by!* She had him all wrong. He'd only accepted the temporary job as a lawman to do Carrey a return favor, not because he liked a structured society with laws or rules. He'd had enough of both as a teenager to last him the rest of his life. Maybe it was a good thing he didn't intend to remain in Calico—not with Leslie as the mayor set on running or controlling everyone and everything.

Jeremy and Tim burst into the room before he could voice his opinion of a highly structured existence and all that it entailed.

"Hi, Mr. McClain! Look what I have!" Tim bounced over to Drew and opened his hand. A fifty-cent piece, damp with sweat, was nestled in his hand.

"Not bad." Drew nodded gravely at Tim's enthusiasm. "What do you intend to do with all that money?"

Tim giggled. "I guess it's really not much, but we have to pay off Mr. Little, just like we promised."

"How about you, Jeremy? How did you make out?" Jeremy, his blue eyes troubled, pulled a dollar bill out of his pocket and shrugged his small shoulders. "I know it's not very much, either. But we needed the money. I guess I'll have to find another job."

"Well, I suppose jobs for kids like you might be hard to come by," Drew answered gravely. "Maybe it would be smarter not to get into debt in the first place."

He waited for the message to sink in. "On the other hand, I think I might have one or two odd jobs in mind. They don't pay much, but every little bit ought to help."

"What kind of a job, Mr. McClain?"

"Whitewashing the shed behind the jailhouse, for one."

"Isn't that what they were supposed to be doing before they made off with the horses?" Leslie interjected. "That's not exactly honest. You don't have to pay them anything."

Drew shot her a warning glance. "Yeah, I know. But since I'm paying, maybe they'll finish the job this time." He considered the interested boys. "How about a dollar an hour for each man?" He could have offered more, but somehow, for his sake and theirs, he wanted their future employment to be a long-drawn-out negotiation. He needed to have an excuse to visit with Leslie.

"Okay," Jeremy answered. He eyed the dollar in his hand dubiously. "It took us all morning to make this much. I guess we'd better get to work."

"Hey, I never said it was going to be easy," Drew answered. After the stupid stunt they'd pulled last night, if the kids thought he was going to take pity on them, they had another think coming. Sometimes the lessons stuck with you when you had to learn the hard way.

Drew pretended disinterest. "When you finish painting the shed, I'm sure I can come up with a few more paying chores. That is, if you want to."

"We want to," Jeremy answered with a sidelong glance at his frowning mother. "When do we start?"

"As soon as those porch railings are back in place. First things first is my motto. Now, give your money to your mother to hold and let's go on back and get started."

In spite of Drew's patient coaching, the boys struggled with one mishap after another. Railings kept sliding over the side and into the gully below. Jeremy dropped a hammer on his big toe and had to stop to take off his shoe to judge the damage. Tim howled bloody murder after he got a splinter in his thumb.

"Maybe this isn't such a good idea after all," Leslie remarked as she stood in the doorway and watched.

"Not to worry," Drew answered as he carefully pulled the splinter out of Tim's thumb. "We're just at the beginning of the learning curve. Come back in an hour and you'll see the difference."

Leslie wasn't convinced, but she heard the tinkle of the bell above the screen door sound as the door opened and closed. With a last doubtful glance at Drew, she turned back to the shop. "Better have Tim come in and wash his thumb with soap and water. The last thing he needs is an infection."

"Morning, Leslie." Keith Andrews, hat in hand, stood smiling at her. "I heard you've called another town hall meeting for tonight. Thought I'd ask if I can be of any help getting things ready.''

Leslie was taken by surprise. It was the first time Andrews had called her by her given name, or even spoken to her directly. Let alone offered to help her. Until now, he'd avoided her like the plague if they happened to meet. She'd seen him look at her with a calculating glance yesterday, then mutter something under his breath. Now, he was actually smiling?

What had happened to make the difference?

''Thank you, Mr. Andrews,'' she answered. She sidestepped him, moved to the quilt frame and pretended to study the pattern of the stitching. ''I think I have everything well in hand.''

''Why don't you call me Keith?'' he invited. ''Surely we've known each other long enough to be on a first-name basis.''

''If you like…Keith.'' She avoided his eyes and sat down to thread a needle. There was something false about that smile of his. Even his manner disturbed her. She was willing to call him anything he wanted if he'd only leave.

''Are you sure I can't do anything to help? In *any* way? I'm yours to command,'' he added suggestively as he stepped in front of her. It was almost impossible for her to ignore him.

''You sure look pretty this morning, Leslie,'' he went on. ''The color of your dress sure goes with the color of your hair. Matter of fact, I'm kind of partial to red hair, myself.'' He started to reach out to finger a tendril that had escaped its braid.

''No, thank you,'' she said firmly as she leaned out

of his reach. "The hall is ready and I have the agenda planned. Maddie has offered to provide cookies and lemonade. I don't see why everything shouldn't go well."

"If you show up for the meeting, this time," Andrews added slyly. "Maybe if we run the deputy out of Calico, you'd have more time for the rest of us men." Me included, said the intimate glance he gave her.

"Mr. Andrews…" Leslie began, refusing to rise to his bait. As far as she was concerned, last night—and her physical reaction to Drew—was a closed issue. And Andrews was the last person she was willing to discuss it with. That, or anything else.

"Keith," he corrected. "I thought we'd agreed to call each other by our first names."

"Mr. Andrews," she went on firmly, hoping he would get the hint that she wanted nothing to do with him. As for continuing to call him by his first name, the only thing she wanted to call him wouldn't bear repeating. She started to rise. "I appreciate your offer, but I've already told you I don't need your help."

"You sure about that? I'd say I'm a big improvement over McClain."

"The lady has already told you she doesn't need your help." Drew strode into the shop, came to a stop behind Leslie and put his hands on her shoulders to stay her. "Why don't you pick up your marbles and go back to the hole you crawled out of?"

Keith Andrews glared at Drew's hands, crushed his hat in his whitened knuckles and taunted Drew.

"What's the matter? Afraid to let Leslie talk for herself?"

"She just did, but you obviously can't take a hint."

"You act like you own her," Keith retorted. "As far as I know from what you said, you don't...not yet, anyway. Besides, you don't even belong in Calico. Who in the hell do you think you are?"

"An interested party, that's who," Drew answered. He was aware he had no right to act this way. Except that he remembered too well Andrews's boast that he could get Leslie to marry him for the reward he thought came with her. And the "pure profit" the louse had hinted at. "And if you don't get your hide out of here in thirty seconds, I'll show you how serious I am."

"Wait a minute!" Leslie shook off Drew's hands and jumped to her feet. Just because they were acting like two dogs fighting over a bone didn't mean she had to stand for it. "I want both of you to stop this right now! I'm not anyone's property, and furthermore, I can take care of myself!"

Andrews hesitated, took a deep breath and started to speak.

"You have twenty seconds left," Drew prompted, glancing at his wrist watch.

"You wouldn't dare!"

"Try me," Drew invited. "Ten seconds."

Leslie threw up her hands. "Mr. Andrews, I think you'd better leave before things go too far."

"How about him?" Andrews gestured angrily to Drew.

"That's my business!"

"Three seconds!"

Leslie folded her arms across her chest and prayed.

With a parting glare, Andrews turned tail and started toward the door. "You haven't heard the last of this," he shot over his shoulder. "Just you wait until the truth comes out, McClain—Leslie ain't going to want to have anything to do with you, either!"

"That's Ms. Chambers, to you," Drew retorted as he started toward Andrews. "And don't forget it!"

The screen door banged shut.

"What did he mean by the truth coming out?" Clearly agitated, Leslie studied Drew. "What truth was he talking about?"

"Nothing for you to worry about," Drew assured her. "He's just blowing off steam."

"You're sure about that?"

"I'm sure," Drew answered. He threw his arms wide and gave her a big grin. "Do I look like I'd tell a lie?"

Leslie wondered if Drew realized that, while he'd made it clear she wasn't going to have anything to do with Andrews, he'd somehow managed to stake his claim to her.

She eyed him carefully. "What brought you inside, anyway? I was doing okay without you."

"Tim came in to wash his hands, just like you told him to. When he heard Andrews get smart with you, he came back out and got me. I was just going to check Andrews out, but it looked as if you might need some help."

Leslie eyed him dubiously. His reason sounded sensible, but there was an undercurrent to his answer. He might have sent Andrews packing, but *he* was still here.

What sixth sense enabled him to be at the right place and at the right time so frequently when he said he intended to leave? she wondered.

Another reason not to trust him.

Chapter Seven

At the stroke of eight, just after the July sun sank below the violet hills, the townspeople of Calico began to gather in the refurbished saloon that was moonlighting as Town Hall. As a concession to atmosphere, fresh sawdust had been sprinkled on the floor. An ancient player piano tinkled merrily in the background. The pungent odor of the freshly built pine benches set up in front of the former bar filled the air.

Leslie nodded her satisfaction as she gazed around her. The hall was ready for business. With the Hullabaloo celebration just two days away, she'd decided it was time for the townspeople to get a few outstanding items on the agenda straightened out. She hoped she'd have better luck with her second attempt—after last night's disaster.

Carrying a large picnic hamper in her hand, Maddie Hanks was the first one through the swinging door. As soon as she spotted Leslie, her eyes began to sparkle with excitement.

"I knew I'd find you here!" Maddie said. She hoisted the picnic basket to the bar with a grunt of satisfaction. "I just met Frank and Herb outside."

"And that was enough to make you happy?" Leslie teased. "You three usually spend most of the time arguing with each other."

"That's only because I keep trying to knock some sense into their heads." Maddie winked. "If they didn't have someone like me keeping them in line, they would have gone to hell in a hand basket by now."

"What was the argument about this time?"

"The fools were taking bets on whether you and McClain would turn up missing for this meeting, too. Since I knew better, I took them up on the bet. I'm going to make a fast ten dollars as soon as McClain shows up." She grinned happily. "Between you and me, I'd already noticed Drew getting ready to lock up the jailhouse and come here. Taking the men's money will be like taking candy from a baby."

Leslie paused in the process of placing copies of the meeting agenda on the benches. "Maddie! You can't mean to do that!"

"Sure I can. Only to teach them a lesson, mind you," she answered in a self-righteous voice, belied by a broad grin. "Some people have to learn the hard way."

Leslie eyed her cheerful friend. With the sparkle in Maddie's blue eyes and her matching powder-blue costume filling out her spare figure, she looked younger than her years. Too bad there weren't any men around Calico with enough sense to appreciate her.

"I don't understand why everyone seems so set on believing last night wasn't an accident. You'd think I got locked up with Drew on purpose! How could you even bet on such a thing." Leslie was chagrined but not really surprised at the way the gossip about her misadventure was circulating. No wonder Keith Andrews hovered around her like a bee over honey; he thought she was ripe for the picking.

One and one was beginning to add up.

"It wouldn't be the worst thing you could have done," Maddie replied, arching her eyebrows. "Why, if I were twenty years younger, I'd be thinking of ways to get holed up with McClain myself."

Leslie smiled at the thought. The idea of Maddie and the much younger Drew locked up together in the shack was too much. "You're incorrigible, Maddie Hanks! If I know you, you'd probably be cooking up a gourmet picnic for the man instead of letting him take advantage of you."

"Maybe not," Maddie answered as she unwrapped the cloth that covered the basket. "On the other hand, the way to a man's heart is through his stomach, you know."

At the thought of Drew's lean, taut middle, Leslie blushed.

"Except, of course, the word's out that you and Drew are more than interested in each other," Maddie continued in an undertone. "Maybe you ought to be more careful about being seen with him. No use looking for trouble."

"Careful? You're not suggesting that I started the whole mess at the cabin, are you?"

"Now, dear, don't get so huffy. I like McClain," Maddie added. "But he did say he's moving on, didn't he? Not that I'm saying he's going to, mind you. It's just that we women have to be careful not to get suckered in by a smooth-talking man.''

Leslie hid a smile at the serious expression on Maddie's face. Maddie was well over fifty, had been widowed for years and had half the male population coming into her café daily. The idea of her fending off an eligible man was amusing. Or was it?

She took another look at Maddie's wistful expression. If ever a woman was meant to fuss over a man, it was Maddie. And if a woman was meant to be a wife, she was it. Leslie herself had made a conscious choice to remain single. But why hadn't she realized how lonely Maddie was under that fierce exterior before now?

Leslie sobered at the thought of being taken in by a man like Drew. Or any other man, for that matter. According to Maddie, men and women belonged together like a platter of ham and eggs. But based on her own experience with her first husband, Leslie knew better. It would take a special man to get her to change her mind about the reliability of men. She hadn't met him yet.

Leslie recalled the night she'd spent alone with Drew and her unexpected response to him. Strangely enough, she had felt safe with him and had even been tempted to live out a fantasy night in his arms. Her senses had cried for something more than a kiss. Until she remembered he had nothing to offer a woman. Not even himself.

She shook the thought from her mind as it occurred to her that Maddie had talked about a bet. Faint bells started to ring. "Wait a minute. Tell me more about the bet."

"Which bet was that?" Maddie asked as she started to unpack the picnic basket. Normally a cheerful, outspoken woman, Maddie suddenly seemed to find something interesting at the bottom of the basket.

"Was there more than one?"

"I already told you," Maddie answered in a muffled tone as she bent over the basket. "Frank and Herb, the jackasses, were willing to bet me you'd get yourself locked up with Drew again tonight instead of showing up here."

"That's all there was to it?"

Maddie, face flushed, looked up and agreed.

"If that's all it was, how ridiculous! You'd think they'd know me better than that by now."

"Of course the whole thing is ridiculous," Maddie said. She lifted out several plates of homemade cookies wrapped in cellophane. Three large glass jars filled with lemonade followed. "I made these cookies myself from a new recipe. They're apple oatmeal."

Leslie remembered Keith Andrews's parting comment that afternoon and Drew's reaction to it. Something was wrong. Why had Drew acted as though he wanted to throw the man out of the door when she'd already told Andrews off?

"Don't change the subject, Maddie Hanks. I'm asking about the bet. Are you sure that's all there is to it?"

"Yes, of course. What else did you expect from men like those two? They don't have anything better to do than mind someone else's business."

"I'm not certain," Leslie answered, frowning at the other woman, who couldn't meet her eye. Betting on a sure thing like whether she and Drew would turn up at the meeting surely wasn't enough to make Maddie act and look so uncomfortable.

There was something more going on than what Maddie was admitting to. And more to Maddie's unease than met the eye.

Before Leslie had a chance to ask, Elias Broome and his wife, Lucy, made their way through the swinging doors. Herb Strawberry was right behind them. "Evening, Ms. Mayor," Broome said as he tipped his hat. "I wasn't sure you'd be here."

"You too? For Pete's sake," Maddie stormed. "Why don't you lay off Leslie? You know as well as I do she had nothing to do with getting herself locked up in the shack with McClain! It was all the kids' doings." Maddie shot daggers at Broome.

"Well, I don't know about that," he answered. "From what Alan told us, she and the deputy looked to be mighty friendly last night." He leered at a blushing Leslie. "Are you sure you and the deputy didn't know each other from before?"

"Before where?" Leslie demanded. She normally prided herself on being businesslike, but lately she was growing angry enough to have steam coming out of her ears. "You know darn well I've spent my entire life in Barstow. McClain is only a stranger who's just passing through!"

"Now, Elias," Maddie warned. "Let's not get carried away. If Leslie says she and the deputy are strangers, then I think we ought to believe her."

"Maybe they were before, but not now," he answered with a calculating glance at Leslie. "Alan swore he saw them in each other's arms making out. Saw them with his own eyes."

"He said wrong," a quiet voice interjected from behind Strawberry and Broome. Drew strode rapidly into the hall. In the silence that fell at his appearance, his leather heels sounded like gunfire. Behind him, small sawdust clouds swirled as he strode. The swinging doors rocked violently back and forth.

"If you can't take my word for it, as a gentleman the least you could do is to take your mayor's." His cold expression and clenched fists invited the man to disagree.

"Yeah, well, I guess you're right. Sorry, Ms. Mayor," Elias apologized under his breath while Strawberry sidled to a seat. Broome tipped his hat and hurried for a front row bench.

Leslie couldn't take her eyes off Drew. As a concession to her request for him to wear vintage clothing, he was dressed in new black twill pants and a long-sleeved black shirt befitting his role as the deputy sheriff, circa 1881. A bolo tie hung around his neck. He wore a new Stetson hat and a leather belt with a wide buckle, just as she'd requested.

Involuntarily, Leslie glanced at his jeans. They were tight where jeans ought to be tight. Shocked at her thoughts, she focused on his boots. Boots were safe. He was shod in new leather boots instead of his usual worn sneakers, and, thankfully, there were no signs of the argyle socks that had offended her.

His expression, as he returned her gaze, was challenging—almost as if he was daring her to comment. She held her breath. He was too sure of himself for her liking. He was too virile. Too male. Except for the lack of a gun belt, he looked like the romantic historic western figure Wyatt Earp come to life, at least as Hollywood had pictured him. He looked relaxed, but Leslie knew better. The man was as angry as a hornet whose nest had been disturbed.

And she was too taken by her own physical attraction to him to do more than hold her tongue. At the rate things were going, she thought in despair, the meeting was doomed before it began. And so was her disturbing physical and mental reaction to the man she'd already decided was someone to beware of.

Leslie forced herself to remember that personal feelings had no place here tonight. She was Calico's mayor, with a position to uphold. The last thing she needed was to fuel the gossip. She had to hide her reaction to the way Drew looked or she'd give herself away. He was already too sure of himself for his own good. And hers. She nodded her thanks in his direction and turned to greet newcomers.

Frank Holliday, Keith Andrews and Alan Little strolled in next. The three glanced silently at Leslie and Drew and took seats behind Strawberry. In seconds the men had their heads together and were casting overt looks at Leslie.

Leslie smiled brightly and continued to hand out copies of the night's agenda. She was all too aware of the speculation in everyone's eyes as they entered. They'd sobered up a bit when they saw Drew lounging by the swing doors, but there was still that calculating look in their eyes. She groaned under her breath. How was she to keep things peaceful with a watchful Drew standing there with folded arms, looking as if he dared anyone to comment about last night? His deceptively lazy stance asked for trouble.

And another thing. She didn't care for the way his gaze wandered to the painting of the naked lady that hung above the bar, either. And definitely not when he shifted and his gaze came to rest on her.

Drew hid a grin. So she'd noticed his contemplative glance at the painting. Her "we are not amused" expression tickled the hell out of him. If she only knew that instead of the voluptuous woman in the painting, he had actually been visualizing the soft woman he'd held in his arms last night. And wondering what it would take to hold her that close again.

Judging from Leslie's look, the woman in the cabin was gone. Tonight she wore a high-necked tailored navy blue blouse and a matching skirt. She wasn't showing an inch of that delectable skin he remembered brushing with his lips as she'd slept. Her eyes were cool, her voice crisp.

So what had made him think she could possibly be the same woman? He shrugged and turned back to watching the people entering the hall.

There were twenty residents present when Leslie moved behind the bar to start the meeting—not nearly enough considering there were twenty-three vintage shops on the main street. Some of the shop owners hadn't even bothered to take her summons seriously.

She began her opening speech by calling the meeting

to order in accordance with Robert's rules of order. Frank Holliday jumped to his feet.

"Heck, we're only a small informal group," he announced. "We don't need all that gobbledygook. I'm all for getting things started."

Annoyed, Leslie shot him a cool look. "Now, see here, Frank, I'm in charge of the meeting. And as long as I am, we're going to do it properly. Lucy, go ahead and read the minutes of our last meeting."

Lucy Stevens slowly rose to her feet. "I'm sorry, Leslie. I guess I forgot to bring them." She sat down amid subdued applause.

"Elias, do you have a treasurer's report?"

"I'm sorry, Leslie. I didn't think anyone was interested—our last meeting was a long time ago."

Leslie sighed. "Then we'll move on to the first order of business on the agenda." She paused to get everyone's reluctant attention. "Now that we have the fire station modernized and this hall refurbished, there are a few other items that need to be taken care of." She surveyed her audience. "So many tourists have discovered Calico, we need to improve the emergency-room service—maybe set up a small clinic. The museum needs some attention, too. We can use volunteer labor again, but we still have to find a way to come up with additional funds."

Greeted by a low murmur, she headed for more turbulent waters.

"I suggest we vote for a one-time assessment to cover costs. Is there anyone to place a proposal for voting?"

Elias Broome jumped to his feet. "Come on, Ms.

Mayor, you know as well as we do there aren't enough of us in town to raise the money to do that. Besides, living here is already expensive enough. Right, folks?" He looked to the rest of the audience for approval. A chorus of assenting voices sounded.

Leslie asked a question to which she already knew the answer. "Do you have any other ideas to raise the funds?"

Paul Stevens rose to his feet. "I move we use the funds from the Hullabaloo."

"That might be an answer—if the celebration makes a profit this year," Leslie replied. "But it'll take a miracle. Besides, there's no use voting on money we don't have in hand. So far, we barely manage to break even."

"Then I move to table the discussion," he answered smartly and sat down.

Lost in reluctant admiration of Leslie's mayoral approach, her pragmatic thinking and her ability to control an edgy audience, Drew wasn't paying much attention to what was going on. As an outsider, the discussion didn't concern him. The next item on the agenda woke him up.

"We might as well move on," Leslie announced. "I intend to set up some ordinances for our visitors to follow."

"Like no spitting on the sidewalk?" Andrews called.

The group broke into laughter.

Leslie managed to smile even though she actually ached to tell him off for not taking her seriously. No one had suggested the job of temporary mayor was going to be an easy one, but the job was beyond belief with a citizenry like this.

"I'm going to set up an ad hoc committee to draft the ordinances," she continued. "Elias, you're the chairman. Lucy, you're the secretary. Herb, Alan and Maddie will make up the rest of the committee unless there are some volunteers."

"I don't think we have time for committee meetings," Holliday broke in. "Hullabaloo is just two days away. Anyway, we're part of the county. Why don't we just follow the ordinances on the books?"

"No one seems to know about them, that's why," Leslie replied. "And no one seems to take them seriously if they do." She pounded her gavel and waited for the hum of voices to subside. "For instance, I'm sure we're all aware gambling is illegal." She paused for effect. "I've heard it's going on right here in Calico." She fixed the men sitting in front of her with a cool stare.

Silence prevailed.

A woman tittered.

Drew straightened up. "Just what kind of gambling were you referring to, Ms. Mayor?"

"I've heard some people are placing bets," she answered with a glance at Maddie. "The subject doesn't matter. Since we're on the road to Las Vegas, I'm afraid some people might stop here and find that sort of thing attractive. I won't allow gambling to spread to Calico."

Lucy Broome stood up. "She's right! If we don't go on record outlawing gambling right now, we'll be in for a lot of trouble."

The men in the audience began to grumble.

Drew stood rooted to the spot. The evening had turned into a period western movie, costumed extras and all. Him included. Soon, he expected, he'd hear a call for temperance and the closing down of Calico's saloons. If Leslie kept this up, the next thing he'd know was that she'd be talking jail terms for misdemeanors, with him as the jailer.

Speaking of bets, he would have wagered his last cent that the one she was referring to was the bet circulating around town concerning him taming her. Or her taming him. He looked sharply at Leslie. Her expression was enigmatic. Nah, she couldn't possibly know about *that* bet. She had to be talking about another one. And, judging from what he'd seen and heard since he arrived in town, there must be plenty of betting going on.

She'd managed to keep her cool so far tonight, but he knew that under that calm façade she wore, she was too serious about her job as mayor and establishing her version of law and order to let the subject of gambling pass. Could she possibly know the hornets' nest she was stirring up? He had to stop her before someone blurted out the truth and all hell broke loose.

Tom Carrey had told him the worst thing that happened in Calico was a tourist getting carried away at the saloon and "jailed" long enough to sober up. Of course, Carrey hadn't been on intimate terms with the Chambers kids or their feisty mother, or he wouldn't have made such a fool statement.

The last thing Drew wanted was for someone to take him seriously as a lawman. If he got himself involved in a court case, he'd have to stick around Calico longer than he'd planned to. Still, a bet was a bet whether it involved him or not.

"Tell you what, Ms. Mayor," he offered. "I'll drive down to Barstow tomorrow and bring back copies of the county ordinances. I'll post a copy in front of this building and the jailhouse. As for the gambling," he added, even though he knew better, "I'm sure we're all reasonable people here. We all know that it's not legal in San Bernardino County. That ought to clear things up." He gazed around the hall, daring anyone to disagree with him. He was gratified to see Strawberry, Andrews and Little squirm on their benches.

"Thank you, Mr. McClain. And another thing," Leslie added from behind the bar, "we have to keep in mind Calico is a California historical monument. We have its reputation to consider. The television and movie companies who use Calico for filming won't have anything to do with us unless we have law and order here."

Drew swallowed a grin. From what he'd read, the town's reputation was light-years away from the one Leslie was referring to. Calico had had more than its share of gunslingers, gamblers and dance-hall girls railroaded out of town. With a fair share left behind to continue to cause trouble. As for gambling, until the streak of silver had run out a hundred years ago, more of it had gone on than Leslie cared to admit.

There wasn't a damned thing she could do to improve Calico's reputation. It was already signed in cement.

"I take it the meeting is adjourned?" he asked politely.

Leslie frowned. "As long as it's understood the committee will meet tomorrow to go over the county ordinances you bring back." She turned back to her audience. "Agreed?"

With their relief showing, the appointed committee members nodded their heads.

They'd agreed too quickly, Leslie decided. She held no real hope they would follow through.

She pounded her gavel on the bar. "Then the meeting is adjourned." She waved to the lemonade and cookies Maddie had set up on the bar. "Maddie brought refreshments. Help yourselves."

For the first time since he'd walked through the swinging saloon doors, Drew was able to relax. Too bad Leslie took the job so seriously, he thought, as he watched her pass out paper cups of lemonade. He had a feeling she'd be a blast if she was ever willing to let herself go.

He strolled over to the bar. "Anything else I can do for you?"

"No, thanks, you've done enough," she answered over her shoulder. Drew didn't know how to take her terse comment, but he was beginning to think he wasn't very welcome here tonight. He turned to leave.

"Aren't you going to try Maddie's new cookie recipe?" Leslie called after him.

"Sure," Drew answered. He paused in mid-stride and turned back to the bar. Maybe he'd been mistaken about Leslie's frame of mind when it came to him. He reached for a handful of cookies, took a bite and grinned. "They're the best yet. A guy could do worse than get used to her cooking."

Maddie preened in the background. Leslie smiled her agreement. "By the way, you look great in that outfit," she added as an afterthought.

"Glad you like it," he answered. Just maybe he'd misinterpreted Leslie. He'd try a light touch and see if it worked. "You might be interested to know, since it meant getting dolled up in a complete outfit that I really hadn't planned on buying, I intend to charge it to Calico's account."

"Not without my permission, you don't," she answered firmly. "I'll have Tom Carrey deduct the cost from your wages if you do."

Drew hid his dismay at the way the conversation was going. Maybe he ought to try a different subject.

"So tell me, what's so wrong with spitting on the sidewalks?"

"If you don't already know the answer, then let me be the first to enlighten you," she replied. "It's unsanitary and very unsightly. And if you try it, as mayor, I'm going to fine you just the same as I would anyone else."

"Hey, lady," he protested. "Maybe you've forgotten *I'm* the law around here."

He crammed his hat back on his head and headed out of the saloon. Damn, he thought, he'd been only trying to kid with her to get her to loosen up. The day he couldn't afford to dress himself would be a cold day in hell.

The way she kept skirting being friendly in spite of his efforts was getting on his nerves.

For the first time, he was willing to believe he'd been mistaken about the real Leslie. She *was* actually a by-the-book authority figure, the kind he'd been avoiding for most of his life. If she had any real passion inside her, she was keeping it well hidden. Any thoughts he might have had of finding the real woman beneath that forbidding façade evaporated. He'd already found her and he didn't like the one he saw one damned bit. He needed to get away from her and out of town.

Leslie watched Drew stride out of the hall. From the way he turned on his heel and jammed his hat on his head, she knew he was angry.

She'd done it again!

He'd been kidding, of course, about charging the clothes and bucking an ordinance against spitting on the sidewalk. Instead of laughing with him, she'd jumped at the chance to put him in his place. Not that she'd meant to—her response had been instinctive. No wonder she had such a terrible reputation. Not that she minded what the men around Calico said, but she did care what Drew thought of her.

She busied herself wiping up the bar and trying to rationalize why she kept responding to him this way.

Granted, he was a cut above most of the men she'd met in Calico. He'd always behaved like a gentleman, even last night when he'd had a chance to take advantage of her fears.

So why had she been so angry with him?

Probably because he reminded her of her ex-husband. He'd turned out to be a traveling man, too.

Or maybe because she'd caught him eyeing the painting of the naked lady hanging above the bar. Not that he was to be blamed for looking. That's what the painting had been put up there for originally. But she'd felt a pang of jealousy just the same.

When his gaze had turned on her, she instinctively thought he was measuring her against the woman in the painting.

Jealous of a painting? How could she have let herself become jealous of a painting of an unknown woman that had hung above the bar for a hundred years?

Maddie had been right about Drew being a hunk. And, in spite of her own resolve to ignore him, it looked as if she'd fallen for the handsome deputy hook, line and sinker.

Chapter Eight

Drew leaned back in his chair, propped his feet on his desk and contemplated the balance of the day still ahead of him.

Before the sun was up, he'd been down to Barstow and picked up a couple of copies of the current county ordinances. He'd also visited the county archives and found a copy of the ordinances that had been in effect in Calico in 1881—the height of its glory days. After he got through laughing, he'd brought back a copy of the list, which might have been appropriate for its time but sounded mighty strange today.

Frank Holliday hadn't been far wrong. "No spitting on the sidewalks" had a prominent place on the list. "No shirttails out on Sunday" and a dozen equally stupefying ordinances followed. But the juiciest one of all was "No visiting Clara Belle's on the Lord's Day, Easter Sunday or Christmas."

Aware that men were men and mining was a lonely business, it looked as though prostitution had been condoned by the powers in charge.

He smiled. He couldn't wait until Leslie saw the list. On the other hand, there was no use adding more fuel to the fire. His smile faded to a scowl. Something more important than the list was nagging at him: his promise to keep an eye on her boys.

One thing for sure was that he had to watch those promises. They were causing him extra work and a ton of aggravation. But as deputy sheriff to the township of Calico, he owed its citizens protection from the Chambers kids.

That thought brought him back to the subject of what to do about their mother.

Leslie. Red-haired Leslie.

He mentally pictured the eligible males he knew in Calico. Next, he deliberately imagined each one of them married to Leslie, holding her in his arms, making love to her. And hearing the sensuous soft sighs she made in her sleep.

He grimaced at the thought. The images were enough to make a grown man cry—especially if the only man he could picture making love to her was himself.

He prided himself on being independent, on not letting any woman hog-tie him or try to regulate his life with rules. And, damn it, that's just what Leslie seemed determined to do. He ought to be fried, but the feisty redhead still filled his waking thoughts and most of his dreams.

He'd always had a thing for red-haired women, although they inevitably spelled trouble. And the name of Leslie Chambers headed the list marked TROUBLE—she and those two kids of hers.

Raising them on her own must take a lot of patience, but that was bound to run out sooner or later. And sure as the fly that headed for him and began buzzing angrily around his nose, it looked as if *later* had arrived. For him, too.

He swatted futilely at the fly, went back to chewing his toothpick and carefully balanced the chair's two rear legs so he wouldn't tip over. But he couldn't take his mind off Leslie. Not even when instinct told him to run like the devil, shake off the dust of Calico and head for calmer pastures.

He looked up when he heard a scuffle at the open door to the jailhouse. Jeremy and Tim, managing to look contrite but not cowed, stood outlined in the sunshine.

If ever two boys needed the firm hand and the guidance of a father, it was these two.

He beckoned them into the jailhouse with a crook of his finger. The way they bravely made their way inside would have been comical if he hadn't remembered the frustration and anger he'd felt at finding himself locked up in the shack with Leslie.

Initially, that is. After he'd made them both comfortable on the narrow cot and taken her in his arms to keep her warm, he'd actually begun to enjoy the situation. It had taken a hell of a lot of willpower to honor his promise just to hold her without trying to make her his. He was pleased with his restraint, but he couldn't stop wondering what if...

"Your mom send you kids over here?"

"Yeah. She said we had to go to work and earn the money to pay Mr. Little."

Jeremy's smile was clearly intended to soften Drew up, but he wasn't in the mood.

"What happened the last time you kids were told to do something?"

"Don't you like us, Mr. McClain?" Tim asked as he cocked his head and studied Drew. A frown crinkled his young forehead.

"I don't know that I do."

"Well, you like our mom, anyway, don't you?"

"She's okay." Drew firmly banished any further sensual thoughts of Leslie from his mind. The way the kid read his mind, it was dangerous territory.

"Cool! Well, *we* decided you liked our mom, even if you didn't know it yet. And since we liked you, too, we thought you'd be happy we picked you to be our dad," Jeremy answered cheerfully. He sobered and took a step backward at the abrupt change that came over Drew.

The last thing Drew wanted was the kids to *like* him.

"I don't want to hear any more of your ideas!" he thundered. "I want action! Or, that is," he amended swiftly, "no more action out of you unless I tell you to. I've had all I'm going to take!"

He caught himself before he went any further. These two were just young boys after all. And he was honest enough to admit his frustration wasn't only with them, it was with their mother.

He tried to remember the wacky things he'd done as a kid. Stunts that had gone over like a ton of bricks. Still, he couldn't remember ever having riled up his uncle or the peaceful citizens of Temptation the way these two managed to do around Calico.

So, what was he to do with the kids?—the answer came to him in a flash. The rodeo!

"Maybe I haven't kept you two busy enough to keep you out of trouble," he said, as he eyed the boys thoughtfully. "I understand you once borrowed a neighbor's steer and were practicing riding him so you could enter the Hullabaloo rodeo."

"Yeah," Jeremy confessed manfully. "But we brought him back."

"Sure you did," Drew replied. "After you let the rest of the cattle out of their pen and sent them stampeding down Main Street. It's a wonder no one got killed."

Drew noted their fading smiles with satisfaction. Maybe they were finally beginning to get the message—they had too many wacky ideas for their own good.

A sometime broncobuster during his more careless days, he was sure he knew just what the boys needed to satisfy their extra energy: mucking out the animal stalls. It was a job assigned to all rodeo wanna-bes to help them decide whether or not to stay in training as riders. More candidates left than remained behind to learn the art.

"I have an idea of my own," he said as he rose to his feet and locked his desk. "Let's go talk to your mother."

"YOU'RE GOING TO DO what?" Leslie plunged her needle into the scrap of material she was appliquéing to a corner of a quilt. "I can't believe you're serious!"

"I am," Drew answered. "I want to take the kids over to the rodeo grounds and see if they can make themselves useful. That is, put them to work. If it's okay with you," he added, hoping to mollify her.

"I don't know," Leslie answered with a frown. "I get a bad feeling just thinking about it. Are you sure that's a good idea?"

What did she expect him to do with the boys—wrap them in cotton?

"It's only a rodeo. The kind where cowboys ride wild horses, rope steers and…"

"Stop right there!" She planted her hands on her hips and glared at him. "I know what a rodeo is. What I don't know is what Jeremy and Tim could possibly do there without getting into trouble! Haven't they managed to create enough problems without you trying to turn them into cowboys?"

"Come on, Leslie," Drew chided playfully. "What do you have against cowboys?"

"Not a thing," she answered with a becoming blush. "Just as long as you don't teach the boys to try to be one. It's too dangerous."

"If I thought it was dangerous, I'd never let them near the rodeo grounds," Drew replied. "I managed to come out whole after riding the circuit, and so will they. It's not as if I intended to let them actually ride the bulls. I just thought they might like to make themselves useful and earn a little money besides."

He'd managed to come out whole all right, Leslie thought, and she swept Drew with a glance that was intended to remind him that he didn't seem to have gotten very far riding rodeo circuits. But all it did was get her imagination going in directions that surprised her. He was *too* whole and *too* all right.

Without shadows hiding the rugged lines of his face and costumed in the same kind of vintage outfit he'd worn last night, he looked sexier than ever. And in the broad light of day, more appealing to her senses than before.

For her own peace of mind, maybe she shouldn't have insisted he dress the part of a nineteenth-century police officer. And as for him being a cowboy, what he couldn't have known was most women were secretly swept away with the cowboy mystique. Including her.

Maybe he was more right than wrong, she decided when she saw the crestfallen looks on her sons' faces. She knew boys had to be allowed to be boys. And mothers had to learn not to be overprotective.

Maybe Drew *was* the sort of man who could show two fatherless boys how far they could go. And maybe if she allowed him an inch he wouldn't want to take the whole mile.

"All right, you can take them over to the rodeo grounds," she agreed. "But only if you keep a close eye on them."

"Cool!" Jeremy answered, his smile restored.

"Yeah, cool!" Tim echoed.

"Okay," Drew said. "But not until you boys promise to stick with me, to do only what I tell you and not go off by yourselves. I wouldn't want you to spook any of the animals—or their riders, either. Agreed?"

He could tell by the way their faces lit up that they thought they'd be riding a bucking bronco. They were in for a surprise.

"We promise," Tim answered. His brown eyes and his feet danced with excitement.

"Jeremy?"

"Sure, me too."

"And I want you boys to stay out of trouble," Drew added for Leslie's peace of mind.

"We already promised we would," Jeremy answered impatiently. "Let's go, Mr. McClain." He reached for Drew's hand and began to tug him out of the quilt shop.

With a helpless shrug of his shoulders, Drew waved goodbye to Leslie and headed for the door before she could change her mind. When he glanced back over his shoulder, he saw her standing there, a half smile on her face.

A smile on her face? And no snide comments about his taking his responsibilities seriously?

It only went to show that if a man didn't try too hard to be friendly, he might get there from here a hell of a lot faster.

"I don't think Mom likes the idea of us going with you one bit," Jeremy announced once they were in the street. "She doesn't like us around animals."

"That include snakes?" Drew said dryly, recalling their snakeskin business venture.

"Yeah, especially snakes," Jeremy agreed.

"Well," Drew offered, "it's time for you kids to learn how to act around all kinds of animals without getting hurt." *Or hurting someone else.*

The doubtful look on the kids' faces turned to hero worship.

Drew realized he'd made a mistake as soon as the

words left his mouth. If he was trying to get their minds off himself as father material, he'd gone about it the wrong way. Sure as the sun would rise tomorrow, they'd set their minds on him as their dad more strongly than ever.

LESLIE STOOD INSIDE the doorway to her shop watching Drew and the boys make their way down the street. She saw him lean over to ruffle the cowlick that was forever falling into Tim's eyes. And then put his arm around the boy. It was a surprisingly affectionate gesture. Strange, since all the man had done until now was to act frosted about being asked to take care of them.

Her mind spinning, she watched while they stopped at Maddie's Last Chance. Maybe she *had* been wrong about Drew. The speed with which Jeremy and Tim had bonded with him should have told her there might be more to him than she'd wanted to believe. Or that she was ready for.

DREW WAITED until they were out of sight of the Quilt Lady before he sprang the next surprise on the boys.

"While we go over to the rodeo grounds, I'd like to tell you about some of the men who used to live in Calico."

The boys cast lingering glances at the road that curved down and around Calico's main street and off into the desert to where the rodeo was being set up.

"Where are they now, Mr. McClain?" Tim inquired politely.

Drew gestured to the hill behind them—the cemetery.

"I don't think I want to go there," Tim announced, pulling back. "Maybe I'll stay right here with Mom."

"We're not going to the cemetery. I just wanted to tell you a few stories I've heard," Drew replied. He was well aware of the stories about graveyards that kids liked to scare themselves with. He'd done it himself. But these weren't going to be that kind of story.

"I thought you might be interested in how many foolish men paid the full price for pulling stupid stunts." When he had their reluctant attention, he began. "The first one was a guy called Cactus George. He liked to play with guns, but he was too slow on the draw." After a pregnant pause, he went on. "And another one was John Smith. Heard he got into a gunfight and forgot to watch his back."

"We haven't shot anyone, Mr. McClain. Honest." Tim's voice hovered on tears.

Not yet, thank the Lord. But a little advance warning couldn't hurt.

"And there were the ones who were more your style," Drew continued. "One was named Hal Thomas. Heard he rode a bucking bronco straight to hell. And, oh yes, there was a J. J. Steele. He used dynamite to blast himself to kingdom come along with his diggings."

"Gosh, Mr. McClain," Jeremy protested, "we wouldn't do that. We were real careful to run when we saw the dynamite was going to explode."

"And I'm sure so did old J.J.," Drew replied dryly. "The point is that dynamite is dangerous and few people know how to use it properly. And that kids should never try to play with it."

"Can we go over to the rodeo now?" Tim inquired in a small voice. "You promised."

"That's another point I want to make," Drew replied. "You shouldn't promise something if you don't intend to keep your word. That's a rule we men have to stick by. If your mom knows you've learned that, maybe she wouldn't have to worry about you so much."

Jeremy nodded. Tim wiped his dripping nose with the back of his hand.

Satisfied he'd made his point, Drew threw an arm over each of the boys to reassure them.

"Now, let me tell you about how I got started riding the rodeo circuit," he started in. "I'd come wandering through town, somewhere in Texas, when I stumbled across the fair grounds and a rodeo in progress. I decided spending some time with real life cowboys would be interesting, so I found the man in charge and offered my services."

"Did you get your own horse to ride?" Tim inquired, his eyes clear and a smile on his face now that they'd left the subject of cemeteries behind. "A real horse?"

"Not right away. You might say I had to learn the business from the ground up before I was trusted with the livestock. You fellows ought to know that. You had a horse once."

"Yeah," Jeremy answered. "Before mom took him away."

Drew smothered a grin. "Why was that?"

Jeremy cast a quick guilty glance up at Drew before he replied. "Mom caught us trying to do trick riding."

Drew wasn't surprised. "Where's the horse now?" he asked, although he already knew the story.

"In Mr. Little's stable. When we took the horses, we figured we were only borrowing back our own horse, Aladdin."

"Well," Drew commented dryly. "Unless Aladdin has a twin, it looks as if you took one of Little's horses too. Like I said before," he went on, "in this part of the country it used to be called horse stealing. You're just lucky Mr. Little didn't want to press charges. Now that I know one of the horses was yours, I can see why he backed off."

"Yeah," Tim agreed. "Mom's only letting him keep the horse until we get some sense into our heads."

Drew wanted to smile, but Tim's matter-of-fact recital of his mother's warning tugged at his heart. He ruffled the boy's hair.

"I don't know about you kids, but *I'm* hungry. How about stopping at Maddie's and picking up some of her apple cookies? Maybe some lemonade, too. Working a rodeo can be thirsty work."

MADDIE LOOKED ON approvingly as the boys made for the large, clear cookie jar that was on the counter. "I knew the boys would get to you sooner or later, just like they have me," she said in an undertone as she poured lemonade. "They're good kids—just need some male attention, that's all."

Drew nodded. "You may be right at that."

"And how do you feel about their mother?"

Afraid of the direction their conversation was taking, Drew glanced sharply at Maddie. "That's a whole dif-

ferent story. Anyway, there's not much point in thinking about her—the lady's made it clear she hasn't any
use for me. Don't know why." He shrugged. "I'm
honest, work for a living and obey the law. I even pay
my taxes like any other decent citizen."

Maddie, who had noted the easy way the boys and
Drew were getting along, stopped to consider the problem. The wry way he'd tried to make a joke of how
he felt told her Drew was genuinely puzzled over Leslie's reaction to him.

By now, Maddie had figured it out. "It's simple,
really. She's so taken up in trying to be a mayor, a
businesswoman and a single mother, she hasn't stopped
to realize she's also a woman."

Drew grinned. "I'll give her that much—she's a
woman, all right!"

"She needs a strong and loving man to watch over
her, take over some of her responsibilities." Maddie
sighed. "But she's too busy trying to manage a life no
ordinary woman, or man for that matter, can handle
alone."

He nodded his agreement. As far as he could tell,
Maddie was right on target in her analysis of Leslie.
Fat lot of good it was going to do him.

"I tried to tell Leslie life is going to be mighty lone-
some once her nest was empty," Maddie added. "But
all she seems to remember is something I told her a
while ago."

"And what was that?"

Maddie paused, looked him straight in the eye. "Not
to let just any man take advantage of her."

"Meaning me?"

"At the time, yes, and I ain't going to apologize for saying it. But I've been thinking on it lately. I've decided Leslie will come to like you once she gets to know you better." She handed Jeremy and Tim a cookie for the road. "Trust me."

Drew tipped his hat, debated whether he should thank Maddie for her encouragement or ignore her advice for his own good, and settled for a quick peck on her cheek.

As they continued down the street, Drew noted the signs advertising gun fights, horseshoe pitching and even a spitting contest over the weekend. Something that would have been forbidden if the early ordinances were to be believed. A stew cook-off was scheduled for Saturday noon, and a barbecue and dance for Saturday night.

After Maddie's words of advice, the event that interested Drew was the barbecue and dance. And only because there was the remote possibility that Leslie might take him up on his invitation if he asked her to go with him. The dance was probably the only way he'd get to hold her at all without starting another argument.

"HI, BEN," DREW CALLED as they reached the worn and well-traveled house trailer that held the rodeo office. The tall, slender and suntanned man coming down the steps shielded his eyes from the sun.

"McClain? Haven't seen you for a coon's age."

"Yeah, I know," Drew replied, reaching to shake the man's outstretched hand. "I've been busy, but I've come to make you an offer you can't refuse."

"That so? You coming back on the circuit?"

"No." Drew laughed. "I'm afraid I've had enough of riding mean horses and chasing spooked cattle. I still have scars to prove it."

Ben Rubard's eyebrows rose as he eyed the gleaming badge on Drew's chest. "That's too bad. You had the makings of a real champion. Going to take up with the law instead?"

"Not exactly. I'm just doing Tom Carrey a favor for a few days." Drew grinned as he pulled Jeremy and Tim around in front of him. "I'd like you to meet some friends of mine, Jeremy and Tim Chambers. Boys, meet Ben Rubard."

Rubard solemnly shook the boys' hands. "What can I do for you?"

"The kids would like to help around the grounds. I figured you'd have something they could do. They come cheap." Drew mouthed that he was paying.

Rubard played it straight. "That so?" He stroked his chin while he studied the kids. "Got any experience with horses?"

"Sure do, both of us," Jeremy replied eagerly. "We used to own one."

"What happened to him?"

Drew intervened. "It's a long story, Ben, and I'm sure you don't want to hear it."

Ben pretended to consider the situation. "How would you two like to help out at the stables? They can use a couple of extra hands."

"They'd be happy to," Drew agreed for his charges. "Won't you, boys?"

"Will we get to ride the horses like real cowboys?"

Ben Rubard coughed to cover up a smile. "Not exactly," he answered.

Drew stepped in to explain. "I think Ben means the job is more like mucking out after 'em."

"Ugh!" Tim wrinkled his nose. "How are we ever going to learn to be cowboys if we can't ride horses?"

"In time, in time," Ben answered in his laconic way.

Drew hid a smile. Ben was a man of few words, but with a heart of gold. He was going to take the boys on.

Jeremy and Tim considered each other, then looked to Drew for guidance.

"It's the only way to learn the business from the ground up," Drew answered casually. The boys had to make up their own minds or the lesson would be lost. "It's up to you. Do you want the job or not?"

"Did you have to muck up the stables before you got to be a cowboy, Mr. McClain?" Tim inquired.

More hero worship! But if that's what it took to keep the boys out of trouble, he was more than happy to go along.

"Can't say I ever made it to a real cowboy stage," Drew answered truthfully. "But yes, I had to muck out the stables, too."

Jeremy straightened up. "Okay, Mr. Rubard. We're ready."

"Follow me," Ben replied and started for the stables. "See you, McClain."

Drew waved goodbye, turned to go and found Leslie watching him from the corral gate. He took a deep breath and strode toward her.

"Checking up on me?"

Leslie surprised him. "Not at all. If I didn't trust you, I wouldn't have asked you to keep an eye on the boys in the first place. I was just curious to see how the rodeo setup was going. It's part of my job, you know."

"No, I didn't know," he answered warily. "Is everything that goes on in Calico part of your job?"

"As a matter of fact, since I'm the mayor, it is," she answered. "Does that surprise you?"

"No wonder you're wound tighter than a drum." Drew's gaze slid over her. She appeared more relaxed than usual—even soft, womanly. "I just wondered if you ever find time for some personal life of your own."

Leslie felt herself blush. Damn, what *was* there about the man that kept her thoughts in a turmoil and her middle in an uproar?

Drew McClain was obviously capable of playing more than one role. He was a wanderer who shed as many skins as a reptile. When he wore the clothing of an old-time lawman, he *looked, acted* and *talked* like a lawman. When he was hanging around a rodeo with all its glamour and excitement, he *looked, acted* and *talked* like a cowboy. And it all seemed to come to him as naturally as the air he breathed.

In either role, he was a man who could have walked out of a woman's dream, including her own. And, no matter how much she told herself to be wary, she was attracted to him. Maybe because her sixth sense told her she had nothing to fear from this man.

It wasn't as if either of them would be interested in a permanent relationship, but being friendly and enjoying herself with him might be a welcome change. If it raised a few more eyebrows, she didn't care. As long as she'd already been tainted with gossip she might as well be hanged for a sheep as a lamb.

Continuing the animal references, she decided to take the bull by the horns and play into his invitation. It *was* an invitation, wasn't it?

"Why? Did you have something in mind?" she asked.

Drew recalled Maddie's parting comment: once Leslie got to know him she'd loosen up. If she'd finally decided to test the womanly waters, he was more than ready to oblige.

"I noticed the posters about the barbecue and dance Saturday night. I was wondering if you'd like to go with me," he said lightly.

"Thank you, I would be pleased to go with you," Leslie answered.

"You would?"

"Yes, I would. What time would you like to pick us up?"

"Us?"

"Of course. Who did you think I could leave the boys with if I date their caretaker?"

From the look on Drew's face, she could tell that taking a woman out on a date with her children in tow was a new experience for him. But the only baby-sitter she'd been able to keep was Maddie, and Maddie was in charge of the barbecue.

A cold feeling came over her. Maybe she'd been wrong. Maybe he *was* no different than the rest of the men in Calico when it came to the boys. She didn't care—her children were more important to her than any man she'd met. "Do you want to take back your invitation?"

"Not on your life," he answered with a lopsided grin that caused her heart to pause in its steady beat. "If I know those kids, they'll find a way to be busy all night. So, do we have a deal?"

"A deal," Leslie answered as she began to envy the woman who would eventually get Drew to put away his wandering shoes. "What time would you like us to be ready?"

His gaze locked with hers, a broad grin covered his face. "Would tomorrow night at six be too early?"

Chapter Nine

Leslie's resistance turned to mush like cookies dunked in sweet coffee. It had been a long time since she'd thought of herself as date material. Drew's invitation was a surprise.

"Six will be fine," she answered, suddenly feeling free and young again. "But I should tell you I've promised to give Maddie a hand. I have to stop by the café first."

"No problem," Drew replied. "We'll go together."

"Well, then, goodbye." She started to leave, then she turned back. "I'm sure I'll be seeing you around before then."

Drew hesitated only for a moment. She'd opened the door and he was ready to accept the invitation. "I was going to hang around here and visit with some friends, but how would you like to have me walk you home?"

"The boys?"

"I can come back for the boys later."

"If you like," she agreed, to Drew's relief. "But I'd like to stop at Maddie's to pick up some scraps of old material for the quilt I've been working on."

"Old material?" He asked the question in order to keep the conversation going and in neutral territory. He enjoyed hearing the sound of her musical voice and watching the shy smile that had come into her enchanting green eyes. It reminded him of his high-school days when girls were girls, not women. And boys were just as shy.

"Maddie discovered some old clothing in pretty good condition in a barrel down in the café's cellar," she explained. "I'd like to see if I can find some antique material to use in the bridal quilt I'm making."

"Got it. I don't mind dropping you off." He offered her his arm and held his breath when she seemed to hesitate. With their friendly rapport so recent, maybe he was moving too fast. Maybe it was too soon to try to be chivalrous. Even though it wasn't a time when men routinely made such gestures, he couldn't wait until tomorrow night to feel the warmth of her against him.

She slipped her hand through his arm, and a dimple danced across her cheek. "Shall we?"

The July afternoon sun beat down as they slowly strolled back up the low hill to Main Street. Heads turned in their wake.

Frank Holliday, Herb Strawberry and Keith Andrews were standing in front of the bank. When they caught sight of Drew and Leslie walking up the boardwalk arm in arm, they began an animated conversation. Andrews became visibly excited.

Aware that they were attracting attention, Leslie had to smile. "I think we've given the townspeople something new to talk about," she murmured.

She was right and Drew knew exactly what had happened. The gambling citizens of Calico had heartburn. Considering how friendly he and Leslie appeared to be, it was anyone's guess who would win the bet circulating through town.

Or had anyone bet that he and Leslie would tame each other?

At the thought, he glanced down sharply at the demure woman on his arm. She was still smiling. No, she couldn't possibly know about *the bet*. If she did, she would have had him railroaded out of town by now.

Maddie beamed as they entered the café. "It's a little late for lunch, but I'm sure I can scare something up for you both if you're hungry."

Drew could tell she was pleased as punch at the way her prediction was turning out—and obviously a lot sooner than she'd hoped. She certainly hadn't expected to see the two of them walk through the café door together only an hour after she'd advised him to have patience in dealing with Leslie.

From the smile that lingered on Leslie's face, he wondered if she'd received the same advice from Maddie.

"What have the two of you been up to?" Maddie inquired cheerfully.

Leslie explained her mission.

"Oh sure. Drew, would you mind going down to the cellar and bringing up the barrel at the foot of the stairs? In the meantime, I'll fix you a ham on rye. Made the bread myself this morning, along with another batch of those cookies you like. How about you, Leslie? The same?"

"Yes, thank you. But I have to get back and open the shop. I have someone coming to pick up a quilt at three."

"Now, remember what I told you," Maddie advised. "No credit cards or checks, especially from strangers. I've had a few checks bounce on me lately, and they were from locals, of all things. I don't know what this world is coming to," she added, shaking her head. "Time was when people could trust each other."

Drew paused at the head of the basement stairs. "Want me to look into it, Maddie?"

"The day you become a real deputy sheriff," she answered with an arched eyebrow. "The way the town is growing, Carrey could use a full-time deputy around here."

There'd been a time when Drew would have been appalled at the thought of remaining in a small town for any length of time. Certainly no longer than it took to clean up, replenish clothing and supplies or to work a few weeks.

He'd sworn off small towns a long time ago. Until he'd run into Tom Carrey and found himself in Calico. He'd expected the short job would be a breeze; instead he'd been dismayed at the unexpected baby-sitting stint he'd found himself accepting. But lately, things seemed to have begun to change.

He made the basement stairs and back in record time. Maddie and Leslie were deep in conversation and giggling like a couple of schoolgirls. At the sight of him, Maddie sobered and began to serve up sandwiches and lemonade. Humming under her breath, Leslie dove into the barrel searching for just the right shade of material. Drew dropped into a chair and studied the two of them carefully.

If he hadn't known better, he would have said he was the victim of another setup. This time by the most unlikely pair of con men, or women, he'd ever come across.

He could believe it of sharp-as-a-tack Maddie. She showed no mercy when she had her heart set on something. Leslie was another question. She was too honest, too forthright to have planned the way things had gone this morning. Until today, she'd acted as if she had been ready to serve his head on a platter if he so much as blinked the wrong way. And yet, overnight, she'd turned into the kind of soft, sweet woman a man dreamt about.

And, strangely enough, it was beginning to look as if whatever waited for him at the end of the rainbow might finally be within his grasp.

It wouldn't have surprised him to find it wasn't any more real than the other rainbows he'd been chasing.

Not that he was ready to reach for it just yet.

HOME FOR LESLIE and the boys turned out to be a small apartment over the Quilt Lady shop. With the stairs hidden behind a closed door inside the shop, he hadn't noticed them before.

"Come on up, Mr. McClain," Jeremy offered when he opened the shop door in response to Drew's ring. "Mom will be ready in a minute. She's getting Tim ready."

"No rush," Drew replied as he followed Jeremy up

the stairs. He waited inside by the door, half listening to Jeremy's chatter about the Hullabaloo celebration.

The apartment was about what he'd expected—three small rooms, an excuse for a kitchen and a bathroom. The narrow windows were curtained in soft shades of lavender, rose, and green. A matching sofa, covered by a handmade quilt, and a few well-worn maple pieces completed the furnishings. Hand-painted pictures, obviously done by the boys at school, were proudly displayed on the wall as if they were treasured masterpieces.

"I'm sorry to keep you waiting," Leslie said breathlessly when she joined him. "We had a little trouble putting Tim together—his good clothes don't seem to fit anymore."

The boys were freshly showered and dressed in neatly pressed jeans and cotton shirts. Tim, tall for his age, had outgrown his jeans, and his white cotton socks were showing. Leslie, dressed in one of those period dresses she wore, looked like a delicate rose. She wore tiny pearl earrings in her intriguing, kissable ears.

"You all look great to me," he answered. "By the way, I've got a little problem, too."

Leslie stopped in the process of gathering up a picnic basket and jackets and paused to consider Drew. He was wearing a trim black suit, crisp white shirt, a red bolo tie and a new Stetson hat. His boots had been newly shined. His deputy's badge was out of sight. He looked more seductive than ever. If he had a problem, it wasn't obvious.

He held out a button and gestured to the third buttonhole on his shirt. "I'm afraid there's been a casualty. Would you mind sewing it back on for me?"

"Of course not—it will only take a minute." She retrieved a sewing basket from a table alongside the couch and motioned him over.

"Would it make it easier if I take off the shirt?"

"No, I don't think so," Leslie replied as she threaded a needle. For her own peace of mind, the memory of what Drew had looked like striding toward her without a shirt the other morning was a sight she couldn't bear to have repeated. Not if she expected to get through the next few moments without blushing her head off.

She slid her left hand through the opening on his shirt. His chest was bare, his skin warm. It took all of her willpower to concentrate on her sewing and not on the taut male flesh heating the back of her hand. The fragrance of his lemon-scented shaving lotion didn't help her sewing either. Especially since the lotion seemed to have taken on some kind of sensual power of its own.

She flashed him an uncertain smile, tightened her lips and her resolve to keep her mind on his shirt and not on the tall, lithe and inviting body underneath. Thank goodness Drew was too busy admiring one of Tim's drawings pinned to the wall behind her to notice the way she felt.

Pretending to look over her head, Drew glanced down at Leslie's shining red hair. Strangely pleased that she hadn't covered it with one of those infernal bonnets of hers, he breathed in the faint whisper of perfume that surrounded her new soft personality. He smiled when he felt her delicate fingers tremble against his skin, jammed his hands into his pockets and hoped she had control of the needle.

This was more like it.

He wasn't even ashamed at the way she reacted when her fingers brushed against his flesh. Or the way his pulse jumped and his skin contracted at her touch.

He had a strong suspicion that this was the true Leslie—and that the mayoral Leslie had worn a mask. He didn't know what had prompted the change in her, but he was pleased. This pert and smiling Leslie was a hell of a lot more woman and fun to be with.

Leslie firmly anchored the button to his shirt and cut off the thread at the knot. "There," she said as she rebuttoned the shirt and patted it in place without looking into his eyes. "It'll never come off again."

"Too bad," Drew drawled, "I kinda like having you put me together."

Leslie straightened. With Drew smiling at her this way, she felt like butter melting on hot buttered toast. The man could move mountains with that smile of his, she thought as she closed her sewing kit with a snap. And furthermore, from the look in his eyes, he knew it.

Now that she'd decided to let herself relax and to try to enjoy their newfound rapport, she found he was making giant inroads into her starved senses and reminding her how much she'd missed. Just the feel of his warm, bare chest against the back of her hand had made her more aware of his innate sensuality than ever—and her own.

She had the uneasy feeling she was being led down

the road of no return. And, to her surprise, she was more than willing to go.

MAIN STREET, never open to vehicle traffic except in emergencies, had been turned into a giant picnic field. Banners announcing the preliminaries of a world tobacco-spitting championship hung over the street from antique light standards. Extra lanterns had been hung across the thoroughfare. A large platform had been built in the center of the street to accommodate musicians and dancers. And, off to one side, by the replica of an old one-room schoolhouse, rides were being set up for children. Down in front of Maddie's Last Chance Café, barbecue drums were already turning dripping sides of beef, pork and lamb. The scent of spicy marinade filled the air.

"Wow!" Jeremy shouted when he spotted the carousel being put together. "Can we go over and watch them set up, Mom? Can we?"

Leslie exchanged a wry smile with Drew. "Yes, but stay in sight. And remember, there's going to be a lot of people milling around soon. I don't want you boys underfoot."

"Promise," Jeremy agreed. He grinned broadly at Drew before he set off for the rides with Tim behind him.

"I guess that takes care of the kids for a while." Leslie looked around at the picnic-goers getting ready to settle down for the evening. "Where should we leave our things? I wouldn't want anyone to come along and help themselves."

"Don't worry," Drew assured her. "I'll leave our

blanket and the picnic basket on the bench in front of the jailhouse. No one would dare rip off anything from right under the law's nose.''

He couldn't possibly be that unlucky, Drew thought. Not tonight, of all nights. Not when he had finally taken a giant step to connecting with the new Leslie. Not when he considered himself free for the evening. ''But I'm not going to worry about it. As far as I'm concerned, I'm off duty. Calico is on its own tonight.''

Leslie didn't look convinced. ''Keeping the law is a twenty-four-hour job,'' she reminded him seriously. ''And don't forget you're all the law there is around here.''

Drew stiffened. This was the old Leslie talking, even if he had to admit she was right. He'd have to keep one eye on the town although he'd looked forward to keeping both eyes on her.

He looked down at Leslie and managed a grin. ''I'll just have to pray that no one gets out of line, won't I?''

Pray? It was pretty clear to Leslie he wasn't only talking about praying for a trouble-free night. The wicked look in his eyes told her he was interested in something besides keeping the peace. Her. Not that she minded one bit. She found herself enjoying every moment of their sexual byplay.

She'd started out determined to show the town that gossip didn't bother her. Instead, she realized as her gaze met his, it wasn't the town she cared about. It was Drew. She was as attracted to him as he appeared to be to her. Tonight, she was doing this for herself.

''I have to go over to Maddie's for a while,'' she

said reluctantly. She would much rather have remained with Drew.

"I can help Maddie too, until the celebration gets under way," he told her. "You didn't think I'd let you do all the work while I watched, did you?"

"Hey, Drew," Maddie hollered from across the street. "Come on over here and open some barrels of apple cider for me."

"Apple cider?" Drew put the picnic basket on the bench and covered it with the blanket. Then he and Leslie headed for Maddie.

"This is a new one on me. I haven't had cider since I left home," he said. He eyed the half-dozen frost covered barrels lined up behind a makeshift bar, inhaled until he was sure the faint tart odor wafting through the air was definitely the scent of apples and not something stronger. Thank the Lord for small favors, it was really apple cider. "Nonalcoholic, right?"

"Of course it's nonalcoholic! What did you think I was talking about?" Maddie demanded. "Hard liquor?"

"No, ma'am," Drew answered, although that was exactly what he'd half expected to find. The night was supposed to be a recreation of an 1880 Hullabaloo celebration, wasn't it? If there *had* been liquor in the barrels, he would have had to pull out his deputy sheriff's badge and close her down. No drinking in public was one of the ordinances on the books.

"Want to be the bartender? Open the spigots yourself? That way you can keep a closer eye on me." Maddie folded her arms across her meager chest and glared at him.

She was daring him to prove her wrong, Drew mused with a chuckle. It was time to put up or shut up.

He couldn't resist teasing a sparkle back into Maddie's eyes. "I intend to keep both eyes open, if only to make certain you aren't up to something shady." He heard Leslie gasp, but he played it straight. "I sure hope the apple juice hasn't been fermenting too long and has a kick bordering on the illegal."

Before Maddie could challenge him, a familiar voice behind Drew turned him around. It was Ben and his rodeo riders.

"Hi, Ben. I'm afraid you boys might be out of luck if you're looking for hard liquor. I haven't made up my mind if these barrels contain apple cider or something stronger." With a broad grin, Drew waited for Maddie to blow.

Maddie lowered her arms. She was looking at Ben as if she'd never seen a man before.

Drew wanted to laugh, but didn't dare. Slim and straight as an arrow, Maddie was a female version of the tall, spare cowboy. When Ben took off his hat and returned Maddie's stare with one of his own, Drew sensed a match made in heaven was being born.

"Maddie, I'd like you to meet Ben Rubard, an old friend of mine. He's with the rodeo. Ben, meet Maddie Hanks. Maddie is the owner of the Last Chance Café and makes cookies a man could die for."

Maddie's complexion, already rosy from the flames of the barbecue, turned fiery red. She wiped her hand on her apron and came around the barbecue drums.

"Pleased to meet you," she said shyly and held out her hand.

Shy? Maddie shy? Drew couldn't believe it. Behind a boisterous demeanor, there obviously was a feminine woman. Including the change in Leslie, that made two women in this town doing their best to hide their femininity.

"Me too," Ben answered, holding her hand for a moment longer than he needed to. "The boys and I thought we'd drop over and see what's going on. Mind if we join you folks tonight?"

Maddie shook her head and for the first time since Drew had known her, appeared to be at a loss for words.

"Why don't you and your men help Maddie out with the cider barrels and a few other chores," Drew suggested. "In fact, Ben, you can play bartender. That'll leave me available to make sure everyone's behaving themselves tonight."

He saw Leslie repress a smile. Of course. He'd just finished praying for a peaceful social night, now he was volunteering for active duty. He winked so that she would know he was diplomatically trying to get Maddie and Ben together.

Leslie added another pleasing facet of Drew's personality to the growing list of things she liked about him.

Maybe she'd been mistaken about him all along. He certainly wasn't the man he'd appeared to be when she'd first laid eyes on him a few days ago. The old Drew McClain would have been long gone by now.

THE REMAINS OF THEIR picnic dinner repacked in the basket, and the boys off to bedevil Maddie and Ben, Drew joined Leslie on the bench in front of the jailhouse. Fiddlers, joined by banjo and harmonica players, tuned up.

Drew glanced down at Leslie. A wistful smile curved her mouth. "Want to dance?"

"I'm not sure I still know how," Leslie answered. "I haven't danced in a while."

"Then it's time to begin again," Drew replied. He took her hands and pulled her to her feet. "It'll come back to you in no time."

"But—"

"No buts accepted, Ms. Mayor." He led her to the dance platform, took her in his arms and lightly touched her French braid. Visions of unbound hair spread over a pillow, auburn on white, stirred his senses. "By the way, do you ever let your hair down?"

"That depends on what you mean," she answered demurely.

"Answering a question with a question isn't exactly fair," he chided. "Come on, what do you have to hide?"

The music started, and he swung them into a country version of a popular waltz.

A surge of emotion filled Leslie at his question. She'd never thought of it that way, but it was true. Determined not to show her pain, she'd been hiding her hurt, her loneliness, behind tightly braided hair and a cool manner. At least, until now. Stronger was better, she'd told herself for the last three years. Until she'd become the ice figure the men in the town had accused her of being.

In Drew's solid arms, she felt all woman again.

"Never mind," he answered. "I was only kidding. I like you the way you are."

The years dropped away as she followed his sure footsteps. Soon, with the firm guiding pressure of his hand against her back, she found herself gliding with him to the lilting strains of the music.

He hummed the familiar melody into her ear. At the moment, he was everything she'd dreamt a man ought to be, a man she could relate to.

They danced several times during the evening, and when the music finally broke into "Good Night, Ladies," Drew took her by the hand and led her back to where they'd left their belongings. As far as she was concerned, the night hadn't lasted long enough. Not when the time spent dancing in Drew's arms had been interrupted by games and a mock gunfight for the sake of the tourists.

She knew he could have done without being asked to referee the tobacco-spitting championship—won by one of Ben's men. Or having to "jail" an exuberant rodeo rider when the guy had produced a bottle of hard liquor and waved it in the air. After he'd read the man the riot act, and the man had passed a sobriety test, Drew had put him in jail, sentenced him to reading the county ordinances and then had come back to let him go.

"I wish tonight could have gone on longer, but I guess it's time to round up the kids," she heard him murmur. "Good thing tomorrow is Sunday and we can all sleep late."

Leslie nodded her agreement, although she wasn't in a hurry to call an end to one of the happiest nights she'd experienced in a long time.

The barbecue area in front of the café had been closed and cleaned up. Deep in conversation, Maddie and Ben were seated companionably on the café's steps. Jeremy and Tim sat drooping at their feet.

Drew chuckled at the sound of his old friend telling tall tales. Maybe the reason Ben hadn't spoken much before was that he hadn't found anyone he wanted to talk to. "Don't believe a word the man tells you, Maddie. He's buttering you up."

Maddie glared at him. "Ben has been a real help tonight. And furthermore, I'm sure everything he's told me is true. For my money, he's the last honest man in the West," she announced with a flourish.

Drew glanced at Ben. If ever a man could blush, sure enough his friend Ben was blushing.

"Of course it is, Maddie. Don't get yourself in an uproar. Now that the dam has been opened, I'm sure Ben has more stories to tell than you're willing to hear. He'll be happy to share them with you, won't you, Ben?"

It was Maddie's turn to blush. "I've invited Ben to dinner tomorrow night after the rodeo contests are over. In fact, he's gonna come to dinner as long as he's in town."

"Good!" Drew winked at the uncomfortable rodeo boss. "Maybe he can extend his stay?"

"Possible," Ben answered, reverting to his laconic

speech. Drew sympathized with him. Poor Ben, he'd probably used up all his strength talking to Maddie.

Leslie bent over her drowsy boys. "Come on, sweethearts, it's time to go home."

"Poor kids, they're already half asleep," Maddie broke in. "Why don't you let them stay with me tonight? That way they'll be handy and ready to go at it again in the morning." She dimpled at Ben. "Maybe you can come and get them and take them down to the rodeo for a while? You can stay for breakfast, if you want."

Ben wanted.

Leslie looked forward to the chance of spending more time with Drew, but she managed not to look too pleased. "You're sure?"

"Sure I'm sure," Maddie answered, getting to her feet. "In fact, Drew can carry Tim in to bed. Ben's the stronger of you two—he can take Jeremy." Ben's grin grew broader.

Since Maddie left no room to disagree, everyone agreed.

"Wait here. I'll be back as soon as I get Tim in bed," Drew told Leslie. "Can't let a lady walk home alone this late at night, can I?"

It was Leslie's turn to color. Home being no more than a couple of hundred yards up the street, she knew she could have made it by herself. But the evening had left her in such a contented and mellow mood, she couldn't bring herself to turn down Drew's offer.

"I'll come along and tuck the boys in bed," she answered. "And then I'd be pleased to have you walk me home." She felt herself dimple at the intimate look

Drew gave her before he hefted a sleepy Tim and followed Maddie into the small house that was attached to the Last Chance.

Tonight was a night to be remembered, Leslie thought as she and Drew strolled up the street. She'd not only enjoyed every minute of Drew's company, she found herself wanting something more.

Drew paused at the door to Leslie's shop. "Would you like me to have a look around before you go in?"

"I've come in by myself lots of times since I moved here two years ago," Leslie said with a laugh. "I don't see anything different about it now."

"It's almost two o'clock in the morning, and the boys aren't with you," he answered. "You never know what kind of critters or snakes could have gotten in while you were gone."

Leslie studied him for a long moment. "You're serious about this, aren't you?"

More serious than she knew, Drew thought as he nodded and returned her searching gaze. Almost overnight, he'd begun to feel an unfamiliar desire to watch over a woman—Leslie. To care for and protect her and to keep her safe from unknown critters or snakes.

Who was he kidding? he added to himself as he watched a strange expression come over Leslie's face. It wasn't critters he was interested in looking for—it was more like looking for a reason to be alone with her without any interruptions. To show her how much he wanted her.

Even though she'd spent the night making tourists welcome, helping Maddie, rounding up Jeremy and Tim from time to time, and dancing with him for hours, she still looked fresh and lovely. He wanted nothing more than to take her into his arms and plant a red-hot kiss on her inviting lips. And, this time, if all went the way he hoped, to spend some time loving her.

"I don't see why not," Leslie finally agreed, "although I'm sure you won't find anything out of the ordinary inside."

When she met his gaze, he knew they both were aware there was nothing alive in her apartment. That he was looking for an excuse to have her alone. At least he was being a gentleman about it—not blatantly manipulative like Andrews.

When Leslie handed him the key, he thought about his own motives for wanting her. It wasn't only for the sexual attraction between them. This was where Leslie lived, raised her rambunctious boys and patiently made the quilts that supported the three of them. She was definitely more than an ordinary woman. If he got the chance, he intended to show her just how much.

Amused by Drew's fake concern, Leslie followed him and waited while he made a thorough check of the shop. To her delight, he headed for the door that led upstairs.

"I really don't think there's anything up there, either," she commented as she followed him.

"You never know," he murmured as he took the steps two at a time.

Leslie repressed a giggle. He was determined to get upstairs. What he didn't know was that she was just as determined to let him.

With the exception of a lamp she'd left burning to

light her way, the apartment was empty of anything that moved.

"Well," Drew said when he finally rejoined her after checking out each room. "I guess everything is okay." He led the way downstairs.

When they reached the front door, he seemed reluctant to open it. He turned to look into her eyes. "You're certain you don't mind staying here alone?"

She shook her head.

"Well, then, I guess I'd better go. Be sure you lock the door behind me." He bent to brush his lips against hers. When she didn't draw away, he put his arms around her shoulders and kissed her more deeply.

"I can't say I'm sorry if I've offended you by this," he told her when he ended the kiss. "I've wanted to do that all night long."

"So do I," Leslie replied. She reached around him and closed the open door.

Chapter Ten

As much as he hungered to believe Leslie wanted him to stay, Drew was afraid to trust his ears.

He'd managed to make a fool of himself before, and he was determined to be mighty careful he wasn't about to do it again. Not after less than two days had gone by since she'd changed from an authoritarian mayor into a warm, passionate woman.

"Are you asking me to spend the night with you?" he asked cautiously.

With a soft smile on her face, she nodded.

He strained to read the truth in her eyes and in the lips that moments before had trembled with passion.

"Are you sure?"

"I'm sure," she answered shyly, reaching to curve her arms around his neck. "For the first time in three years and more than ever before."

He held her close, felt her rapid heartbeat against his chest. If there ever was a time for him to face the truth, it was now.

Leslie was too special a woman to toy with for a few days. Or longer if he decided to remain in Calico after the Hullabaloo celebration was over. And, if he became restless again, much too special to leave behind when he moved on.

Now that he was beginning to know the real woman under the mask, he knew she was too fine a person, too caring a woman, to hurt. If he had any smarts, he'd let her go. But he couldn't, not just yet.

He held her to him for a long, precious moment, enjoying her scent, her soft and curvaceous body as she clung to him. He finally took a deep breath and moved with her inside the shop.

"I think it's time to talk things over before it's too late."

Leslie looked confused. He didn't blame her, he was having trouble keeping his thoughts coherent, too. Talking was the last thing he wanted to do, but he was driven to be honest with her.

"Did you say you wanted to talk?"

He pulled her closer with a wry smile and kissed the tip of her nose. "Maybe it would help if I used the word 'explain' instead. There are things you need to know about me before we go any further."

"Drew," she protested, running her fingers lightly across his lips. "There's nothing to explain. I know what I'm doing." A becoming pink tinge came over her face. "I *have* been married before."

He raised his eyebrow at her remark. Leslie might not be a novice in the game of love, but she sure behaved like an innocent. Didn't she know sex and making love weren't always the same thing? It was time to explain the difference.

He took her fingers between his lips, kissing the tip

of each one tenderly. "That's not exactly what I meant."

"Then I don't know what you do mean," she said, looking more bewildered than before. "Surely, all there is to know is that we want each other?"

"No, sweetheart," Drew said gently. "Tonight is going to be more than that. But first, I'm trying to be up-front with you."

"Are you trying to tell me you don't want me?"

He felt like a heel when she pulled away. "Almost more than life itself," Drew answered, trying to coax her back with a smile. "It's because I do care for you that I want to be honest with you."

He held his breath until she came back into his arms. What he had to say didn't come easily, but he had to say it now if he was going to be able to live with himself later. If he had his way, tonight was going to be a night they both would remember.

"This is the first time in my life that I've wanted to explain myself to a woman," he began. "It's because I care about you that I have to do it now. I don't want to do anything to hurt you."

"Hurt me?" She searched his face, doubt surfaced in her eyes. "Surely loving me can't hurt me?"

Drew gently stroked the soft, velvet skin of her throat. "I guess the only way to tell you how I feel is to come right out and say it." She nodded, and he went on, "If what you mean by loving you is to make a commitment to remain with you forever, to be a father to the boys, I'm afraid I'm not the man for you."

He gestured around the room, to the drawings on the wall, the scarred coffee table covered with comic books. "This is your kind of life—settled, sure. And so is your knowing where you're going to wake up tomorrow. I'm not certain your way could be mine."

"I thought you cared for me," she whispered. "Was I wrong?"

"I do care for you, very much. In fact, to be honest with you, the idea of caring for someone like you is new to me." He hesitated, knowing the next few moments were critical to their relationship. He didn't want her to take him wrong, but he had to be honest with her no matter what the price. After tonight, there would be no going back to their old relationship of mayor and deputy as long as he stayed in Calico.

"But if by loving you, you mean having you welcome me with your soft, open arms as long as I'm here, then I'm yours."

"I'm not sure I understand what you're driving at," she murmured into his throat. "And I'm not sure I want to try."

"I'm saying I can't make you the promises of a tomorrow you deserve to hear," he added with regret. "Not yet, and maybe never."

His confession was the most difficult thing he'd ever had to do. Knowing that he might be hurting her even more by telling her the truth was harder yet.

"I haven't asked you for any promises," Leslie answered. "The truth is, tonight was so wonderful I didn't want it to end."

"I know," he answered, "and neither did I." Frustrated, Drew gently rubbed the nape of her neck. He might be a traveling man, but he'd always prided himself on being honest. Even if the chance to make love to Leslie slipped through his fingers. "It's just that I know women like you tend to play for keeps and that men like me tend to get restless."

"If so, then I suppose we'll have to make tonight last forever and a day," Leslie murmured, reaching to unbutton his shirt. "Tomorrow can take care of itself."

She could feel his muscles tense as she continued to slip open the rest of the buttons of his shirt. She loosened his bolo tie, urged him out of his jacket. With a quick, provocative glance into his eyes, she began to tug at his belt.

She could feel his desire strain under his tight jeans, aching for fulfillment. Her own desire for him heightened. Frustrated, she chided herself when the buckle wouldn't give. Now was no time to give up. Not when she wanted him so. She tried again.

"Better let me help," he said. "Those western belt buckles sure are murder to open when you're in a hurry, but the boss-lady ordered me to wear it." His fingers danced with hers until all the nerve endings in her body began to tingle.

"She couldn't have known how difficult it would be at times like this, or she wouldn't have been foolish enough to insist you wear it," Leslie commented fiercely under her breath. Every time she thought she had the buckle undone, his fingers got in the way. She had a growing feeling that he was deliberately hindering her progress. Was it to get even with her because she'd ordered him to dress this way?

She was beyond the point of wanting to play games. Finally giving up, she stepped back and glared at him. "I guess you'll have to take it from here. That is, if you mean business."

"I mean business, all right," he teased. "I just wanted to see how far you were willing to go to remain in charge."

She waved away his comment with a frown. "Drew McClain, if you don't start to cooperate, you're never going to find the answer!"

"Why don't you let me unbuckle the belt?" He smiled. "From what I can remember, it's a man's job. And so is this." He undid the buckle, reached for the opening on her starched lace collar and slowly undid the pearl clasp.

When his fingers caressed the flesh at her throat and dipped down to the tender spot between her breasts, shivers of anticipation ran through her. Surely heaven couldn't possibly be any better than this, she thought dimly when his hand cupped and played with an aching breast. Not unless Drew would be there with her wielding his magic.

"And this," he added as he slowly slid the bodice of her dress off her shoulders. The friction of the starched cotton material on her newly awakened skin made her squirm in heightened desire.

The ties on her camisole were next.

Undressing her turned out to be a slow striptease— with stops in between each time she reached out to make sure he was real. He was. He responded with another deep kiss every time she touched him. She closed her eyes, tasted him as he tasted her, and drank in the male scent of him.

When he placed a series of lingering kisses along

her breasts, she almost stopped thinking at all. She only knew she wanted to lose herself in this man who had appeared out of nowhere to turn her into a real woman again.

Maddie had been right, Leslie thought while she was still able to think. She *had* forgotten what it felt like to be a desirable woman in the arms of a man, especially if she was crazy enough to think she loved him. Drew was a man who had seen the real woman beneath the cool shell she'd created for herself. He'd recognized her need to have a man to love and cherish.

Somehow, she found herself on her bed. She gazed at Drew through lowered lashes while he finally undid the ridiculous buckle. How foolish she'd been to order him to dress as if he were an actor on a stage.

He'd worn his innate masculinity like a cloak, but she'd been too set on keeping control of her surroundings to see he had no need to pretend to be a real man—nineteenth-century or not.

"You're thinking again," Drew chided as he reached in his pants pocket, removed a small foil packet and put it on the maple nightstand. "I don't want you to think," he said as he rested a knee on the side of the bed and leaned over her. "I want you to let yourself go and to feel. To feel with your heart instead of your head. I want you to forget everything and everyone. I want you to be my woman tonight."

She could see his heart's message in his eyes. She opened her arms and held him close when he finally joined her in bed. He was right. Tonight was a time to turn half-forgotten dreams into reality. To live only for the moment. Nothing else mattered but the man she'd chosen to free her of the past.

He was heavy and solid and all male as he lowered himself into her arms. Moonlight streaming in through the window revealed intense brown eyes that pierced her with hot desire, lips that curved in a tender smile. She reached for him and gently caressed his lips, his cheeks, the nape of his neck, and lifted her lips for his kiss.

He obliged her with a kiss that seemed to delve into her very soul. His hands roamed over her, passionately kneading her flesh and then soothing her to take away any hurt. She moaned, her breasts aching with the need for his lips to satisfy the tension building inside her.

He seemed to understand. With a gentle murmur, he kissed her breasts again and again until she pulled him closer still. Murmuring his desire, he rose over her and slowly made them one.

Lit by a benevolent moon, the velvet darkness that filled the room split into a thousand shimmering silver pieces. If this wasn't loving, she thought dimly before she was swept away by a rising tide of sensuous emotions, she didn't know what else to call it.

DAWN CREPT INTO THE ROOM, the dim light from the awakening morning flickered through gently blowing curtains. It took Drew a few moments to remember where he was and that there was a glowing woman in bed with him.

It wasn't a dream, as he'd first feared. He knew, looking at a sleeping Leslie, that the night had been real and more than wonderful. Never in a million years would he have believed Leslie would give herself to him—and in such a loving and generous way—especially after the way they'd first met. Nor that he could lose himself so completely in her arms.

He wasn't sure what caused the change in her, but he'd treasure every moment of it.

Almost afraid to believe the truth, he examined Leslie more closely. Her hands pillowed her cheek, her shapely legs were drawn up against her middle. She looked lovelier and more appealing than ever.

With a tender smile, he gently drew her to him and covered them with the comforter. For only a few moments, he told himself. He had to leave before daylight found him.

He thought of the night they'd spent together in the miner's shack when he'd awakened to find them cuddled together like a pair of spoons. He hadn't been able to do anything about it then, not after he'd promised only to hold her. And not with the kids and Alan Little staring at them. But the night had filled his heart and soul.

This time, she'd given herself to him in a way more incredible than he ever could have imagined.

In the early morning light he found she had dimples at the back of each of her shoulders. He was bending to kiss them when she stirred and nestled closer to him.

He could tell from the pause between awakening and realizing she was in his arms that she was just as startled to find them together as he had been when he'd first awakened. With a soft laugh, he lifted her face and kissed her half-closed eyes. "Good morning, sleepyhead."

Wide-eyed now, she covered her lips with her hands. Her enchanting embarrassment at finding them in bed together showed. He had to do something fast to ease her discomfiture. And, if time permitted, to make love to her again.

"Second thoughts?" he asked, all the while hoping he was wrong. The last thing he wanted was Leslie to regret having asked him to spend the night with her. Not when he fervently hoped she would ask him back again.

"No," she answered with a small, rueful grin. "It's just that I'm not used to finding a man in my bed in the mornings. Nor at any other time," she added quickly before he had a chance to speak. "I hope I haven't given you any wrong ideas."

She didn't have to worry. From the moment he'd taken her into his arms last night, and long before she'd invited him to spend the night with her, he'd sensed her sweet innocence. It had been almost as though she was virginal, and in some delightful ways, she had been.

The knowledge that he'd been the lucky man to awaken her sensuality made her more precious to him than ever.

"I have to leave soon, I'm on duty," he reluctantly told Leslie. "But not without a last kiss."

He pulled down the comforter, gazed in fascination at her body. He'd thought he'd explored every inch of her, but on closer inspection, there seemed to be a few spots he'd missed.

"You're very beautiful, and I'm afraid I can't stop showing you how much. Especially here and here." He went on to demonstrate with a kiss. One kiss followed another, until she surged into his arms.

"Don't stop. Show me again."

The crimson tide that came over her as he bent to his task pleased him no end. That he had the ability to cause it pleased him even more.

He stole a quick glance at the clock beside the bed. If he'd had his act together, he would have left by now. But, come hell or high water, he couldn't bring himself to do it. He would have had to be made of iron to leave Leslie and go back to his empty one-room quarters beside the jail. The truth was, he was only flesh and blood.

Silently, he lowered her back to the bed. He saw the answering need in her eyes and kicked away the comforter so he could see more of her. "You're right. There *are* a few spots I must have overlooked," he assured her. He demonstrated with another kiss at the hollow between her breasts, at the nape of her neck, on her delicate earlobe.

"If I remember correctly, that's actually the umpteenth time around," she laughed. "No fair. It's my turn."

It took all of Drew's self control to lie still while Leslie covered him with featherlike kisses. When she lingered at a particularly sensitive spot, she was asking for more than a man could take.

He caught her in his arms and flipped her back onto the bed. He covered her body with his own and held her hands at her sides. "Now you're going to have to pay for what you started," he told her with as stern an expression as he could muster. When she returned his gaze with a knowing one of her own, he spread her legs apart with one knee and slowly lowered himself into her warmth. Her cries of pleasure fanned already lit flames. The time and the need for caution faded away.

Later, much later, he grinned at his naiveté. He should have known a warm and willing Leslie would be too tempting. And too smart to let him leave before she was ready.

THE SUN WAS ALMOST UP when he strode down the street to the jailhouse. In less than an hour, the citizenry would be making preparations for a flapjack race—the winner to be awarded all the flapjacks he could eat. Knowing Maddie, she would press paper platters of flapjacks and syrup on everyone as long as they were able to hold a fork.

The dance platform had been cleared to make way for arm-wrestling contests and the finals of the world tobacco-spitting championships. In the distance, he could hear the warming-up sounds of the engine of the miniature train that took tourists on guided tours through a silver mine.

It was later than he'd thought. But Leslie had been irresistible in her desire for him, and he had been more than willing.

His hand froze in the process of unlocking the door to the jail.

Pinned to the door was a Polaroid snapshot. Someone had caught Leslie and himself on film last night. They were locked in an embrace at the open door to her shop. Her arms were around his neck and they were exchanging a torrid kiss.

The snapshot clearly showed it had been in the dead of night. The abandon with which they were kissing told the whole story.

It didn't take a genius to conclude he and Leslie were about to enter the shop together. So what was wrong with opening the door to her shop? he thought defensively. Nothing, unless it was a clear prelude to a night of loving, came the answer. For sure, someone had jumped to that conclusion or the photo wouldn't have been pinned on the door.

He could visualize Keith Andrews, for he'd seen the creep taking Polaroid pictures of the tourists. He'd waited until it had been obvious Drew wasn't going to leave Leslie anytime soon to snap them.

With his luck, the guy would probably arrive shortly and demand to know who had won the bet.

As far as Drew was concerned, if one considered the nature of the bet, it had been a draw. Not that he'd been trying to prove anything by spending the night with Leslie—he'd deck the man who said so. But it was the word of Andrews against his own. Drew wasn't sure how many betting citizens of Calico would believe him. Except Maddie, of course.

If he didn't have to shower and change and check on Jeremy and Tim as he'd promised Leslie, he'd rout out the man who was too cowardly to confront him in person.

But there were still the remaining contests and the rodeo to keep an eye on. The bastard would have to wait his turn.

"Good thing you showed up, McClain," Maddie announced with a theatrical frown. "Those two boys of Leslie's are eating up the flapjacks faster than I can make 'em!" Behind her, Jeremy and Tim were enthusiastically downing a short stack dripping with maple syrup. Their milk glasses were empty. Neither looked ready to quit eating.

It didn't take a genius to realize Maddie wasn't kidding. Not when he saw Ben Rubard hurrying up the street. He recalled that Maddie had invited Ben to breakfast. The man couldn't wait to get started and it was obvious Maddie couldn't wait to get him alone.

It was time to start the boys moving so that Maddie could devote herself to fattening Ben up before the contest started. As for Ben taking the kids back to the rodeo, he probably would forget that as soon as Maddie set her eye on him.

"Come on, you two. Get your gear together and let's get you home before your mother starts to worry."

Not that he believed she would. When he'd finally left Leslie burrowed into the comforter, she looked as if she could sleep all morning. Maybe he ought to take his time walking the boys back home and give her some needed R and R time.

Too bad he couldn't have stayed with her. There must be some spots to explore he'd managed to miss.

On the way back, he spotted Herb Strawberry putting out reproductions of the old Calico *Gazette* with its 1881 headlines. In Drew's opinion, Strawberry was a man only a few cuts above Andrews, and that didn't say much for him. But to give the man some credit, while he'd been in on the betting, he hadn't made a play for Leslie. At least not that Drew was aware of.

"Do you have a minute, Herb?"

Strawberry looked over his shoulder at Drew and shook his head. "Not much more than that. Make it quick. I've got a lot of things to do this morning."

"Then I'll come straight to the point," Drew assured him. "I'd like to know just how far that bet of yours has gone."

"Bet? What bet are you talking about?" He took a quick glance around. "There isn't any bet. You know danged well our mayor spoke out against betting the other night."

Even with his faked affront, Strawberry looked guilty as hell.

"Come off it, Herb. You and I know there's a bet going on concerning Leslie and me. I want to know who else is involved and how far has it gone?"

Strawberry hesitated. "Are you asking me as the deputy sheriff?"

"No." Drew looked him straight in the eyes. "Man-to-man."

"Well, in that case, I guess it's all right to tell you. It's most of us men against a mess of women Maddie recruited." He leered at Drew. "So tell me, who's going to win?"

Drew wanted to tell him what he thought of the bet and everyone else involved, but he'd found out what he wanted to know—Herb wasn't in on the Polaroid caper and Andrews hadn't yet spread the word about what he'd seen the evening before.

That meant only one thing—last night Andrews was in it by himself. And Drew hated to think what had motivated him.

"Save your money, Herb. It was a fool idea in the first place. I told Andrews and I'll tell you, I'm not going to be around much longer to settle the bet one way or another." Drew cursed under his breath and stalked away before he gave in to his anger, leaving Herb staring after him.

The more Drew dwelled on it, the thought of walking away from Leslie had less and less appeal for him. The idea of staying and protecting her from scum like Andrews had taken root and was growing like a newly seeded spring garden.

How could he move on and leave her to face the gossip if Andrews showed off the Polaroid snapshot? How could he think of leaving before he found out what it was that Andrews was cooking up?

He remembered the time he'd found Andrews in Leslie's shop bedeviling her with some fool offer she hadn't wanted to hear. He'd had to practically throw the man off the premises to get rid of him. It didn't take much imagination to realize Andrews was the kind of guy who would try to get even.

He didn't care if Andrews tried something with him. He'd tangled with scum like him before and he knew just where it hurt. Leslie was a different story.

She was too vulnerable right now to leave her on her own.

The least he could do was hang around after the Hullabaloo was over and things had settled down. And not leave before he straightened out Andrews and anyone else who behaved as though they might hurt Leslie.

HE STOPPED in front of a shop whose new sign proclaimed it was the best place in the West to pan for gold. Gold? Hell, everyone with an ounce of brains ought to know Calico had been silver territory during its heyday. What little gold that had been found wouldn't even have excited a dentist's convention. And after the silver mines had run dry, even digging for the white crystalline borax hadn't proven profitable.

With no way to prosper, Calico had shut down until someone had come up with the bright idea of turning it into a tourist attraction.

He gazed at the miniature train chugging along behind the buildings across the street, taking its first load of tourists into a showcase mine. As far as he could tell, the only money still to be made in Calico came from trading on its past.

Leslie had been right in insisting that he dress in costume and act as if this were still 1881. Modern enterprise didn't stand a chance around here.

He smiled at the memory of Leslie and how she'd looked when he'd left her snuggled in bed after a final kiss.

His smile faded when the vision of her lying there pink-tinged and sleepy from their night of lovemaking grew more clear. He'd been so involved in making love to her he hadn't thought about it until now.

Even in the midst of passion, Leslie hadn't let down her hair!

Was there still some part of herself she'd kept hidden from him?

Chapter Eleven

Drew thought about Leslie's tightly braided hair with a sinking feeling.

He should have known the abrupt change in Leslie's demeanor, from cool to red-hot, had been too good to be true. Not that he complained about the way she'd given herself to him so freely. She'd met him with the same fierce desire, matching kiss for kiss, touch for touch. Together, they'd plundered depths of sensuality that had left him breathless.

Both in bed and out, she was everything a man could want in a woman.

And yet, although she might have been honest in her passion, her tightly braided hair told another story. Had it been a subconscious signal there was still something about him that bothered her? Or was there still a part of her she was keeping to herself?

He'd taken a risk in being up-front and honest with Leslie before he'd taken her in his arms and shown her how much he desired her. He'd even been frank about his past and uncertain future. Why couldn't she have been as honest with him?

The closer they became physically, the wider the chasm seemed to grow between them.

He could take anything except not being trusted, or not accepted for himself.

He jammed his fists in his pockets and strode down the street just as Alan Little brought out his miniature ponies for children's pony rides.

"Morning, Deputy! Don't forget you have to judge the finals of the tobacco-spitting contest!"

Drew halted in his tracks. "Why me again, for Pete's sake? Wasn't last night's preliminary enough? I don't even like the smell of tobacco, let alone having to watch the chewing and spitting."

Little scratched his head and finally came up with an answer that pleased him. "Because you're the law, that's why. Last year's contestants were about to shoot the guy who volunteered to be the judge. Didn't the sheriff tell you about it?"

"No, he didn't tell me I'd have to keep the Hulla-baloo contest participants from killing each other," Drew said as he eyed the preparations for the contests. "He only said he wanted me here to keep an eye on the celebration." Nor had he told him what to expect from Calico's lady mayor, her kids, or the type of "businessmen" he would run up against.

If you could call them businessmen, Drew pondered with a scowl. In his opinion, most of them were retired men ready to bet on everything from the size of a gnat's eyebrow to whether Drew would tame Leslie before she managed to tame him. They obviously weren't busy or serious enough to stay out of someone else's business. In Keith Andrews's case, everything moving seemed to be fair game.

No wonder Leslie had asked Tom for help and Tom had hired him to do the job. She obviously felt she couldn't take on Calico and its odd assortment of citizens by herself, and she'd been right.

Maybe fate had brought him to Calico.

"You *are* going to judge the spitting contest, aren't you?" Little let out a squeak when one of the ponies, tired of being ignored, tried to take a bite out of his rear.

"Okay, I'll be there." Drew sighed. Just his luck. Hullabaloo took place once a year, and he'd had the misfortune to land smack in the middle of it.

"And don't forget the arm-wrestling contest!" Little called after him.

"Anything else?" Drew inquired. He could hear the sarcasm dripping from his voice, but he was beyond caring. At the rate things were going, he'd be too busy to escort Leslie over to the rodeo as he'd promised.

"Nope," Little replied cheerfully, rubbing his posterior. "Doc Parsons is going to judge the flapjack race. Last year, the runners ate so many of the flapjacks they all got sick and no one could decide who won. Doc said he might as well be the judge so he could be handy if it happened again."

"Thank heaven for small favors!" Drew grumbled.

In spite of the warm wind that was blowing through Calico, he headed for Maddie's and a hot cup of coffee to clear his thoughts.

He wondered if he could ask Leslie about his uneasy feeling she was holding something back. He'd look pretty stupid if he complained about her hair remaining braided throughout the night. She'd probably ask him why he hadn't taken the initiative and taken down her hair if he felt that strongly about the way she wore it.

The truth of the matter was that she would have been right. Any red-blooded male would have undone her braid and spread it over her pillow the first thing. He'd thought about doing it often enough, himself.

Hell, he'd been too busy loving every inch of her to think of her hair. It had been broad daylight before he'd realized she'd worn it tightly braided as usual. The braid seemed to have become, in his mind at least, synonymous with a suit of armor.

He saw Keith Andrews come out of his photography shop and stand at the door. He was dressed as a nine-teenth-century dandy, bowler hat, cane and all. From the self-satisfied smile on his face, the guy was aware he was drawing second glances from the female tour-ists browsing up and down the street. Now was as good a time as any to confront Andrews with the Polaroid shot that had been left on the jailhouse door.

"You must have been busy last night taking pictures of the goings-on?" Drew asked.

Andrews tried to look important. "You might say so. After all, taking pictures *is* my business."

"Including the shot you took of me last night?"

Andrews's smirk disappeared. A wary look came into his eyes. Drew wasn't fooled. The guy looked guilty as hell.

"I don't know what you're talking about."

"In that case, I guess you wouldn't know what I'm

talking about if I told you I'll skin you alive if you show the shot to anyone but me, would you?''

"That depends on you, McClain.''

Drew knew his instinct had been right. He'd always been able to smell a polecat a mile away, and Andrews was a ripe example. "Yeah? How?''

"If you don't stop getting between me and the lady, I just might show the shot to interested people.'' The smirk was back on Andrews's face.

"I'll give you some credit for realizing Leslie *is* a lady,'' Drew replied angrily, "but that's the only thing in your favor. Too bad you don't have the sense to leave her alone.''

"Oh yeah? That's as much as you know about us. Maybe Leslie doesn't agree with you!''

"I didn't know there was an 'us.' '' Near the end of his rope, Drew narrowly managed to keep his temper. His fingers itched to teach the guy a lesson he'd never forget. If only they weren't standing on Main Street in full view of the awakening town. Unfortunately, it was his responsibility to keep the peace.

"There would be if you weren't always hanging around her, getting in the way!'' Andrews answered petulantly. "Of course, now that I know she's made herself available, I figure it's only a matter of time before it's my turn.''

Drew leaned close to the man's face. "Look at it this way, Andrews. As near as I can tell, Leslie's made it clear she doesn't want any part of you. I suggest you wise up and leave her alone.''

"Hell, I intend to marry the lady!'' Andrews answered. "That's more than you can offer her.''

Drew caught his breath, and his stomach churned. The guy was right. Marriage hadn't been on his mind, not even after he became attracted to Leslie and her feisty ways.

He considered the look of triumph on Andrews's face. The guy was rotten to the core, his plans for Leslie included. Even if he somehow managed to talk her into marriage, she was much too good for the likes of him.

The danger was that Leslie had obviously mellowed. What if she hadn't discovered Andrews and his miserable plan to marry her for the reward or the vein of silver he thought came with her? What if, in her present state of mind, she wanted to be a wife again and Andrews was in the right place at the right time?

Drew's pulse soared at the picture of the warm and passionate Leslie in anyone else's arms but his own.

"In a pig's eye," he retorted. "Keep on talking like that and maybe I won't be going anywhere after all!"

"You will when I get through telling Leslie the bet was your idea," Andrews blustered. His celluloid collar dug into his reddened cheeks. "And after last night, I've just about made up my mind to tell her!"

Drew was struck with impotent fury. He'd sworn to uphold the law—the last thing he could do was pick a fight with the guy. "You know damned well I wasn't in on the bet, let alone the one who thought it up!"

"Maybe, but by the time I get through sweet-talking Leslie, she'll believe anything I tell her."

"You don't have that kind of nerve," Drew challenged.

"Sure I do. And she'll believe me. After all, I'm an

upstanding businessman with roots here in Calico. You're nothing but a stranger passing through, and she knows it.''

Drew clenched his fists, knowing the guy was right—at least about Drew being a stranger. Was it his itchy feet that bothered Leslie last night? Was that why she'd kept a part of her to herself?

He tried to remember what he'd told her. Maybe he'd been too honest about his wanderlust. Maybe he should have kept the door open.

''You won't be able to get out of town fast enough when I get through with you,'' Andrews continued. ''The only reason you talk so big now is because you're wearing a lawman's badge.''

''I can take it off any time you're ready,'' Drew answered. He reached for the badge pinned to his vest, clenched his fists, ready to take the guy on.

''You wouldn't dare!'' Andrews's handsome features became mottled with anger.

''Try me,'' Drew urged him. ''Just go ahead and try me.''

The photographer's eyes spit hatred. That was okay too. Drew understood hatred. What he didn't understand was how the guy could stoop so low as to propose marriage to a woman like Leslie for monetary reasons.

If the poor sucker only knew the reward was nothing more than a twenty-dollar bill. And as for the small streak of silver that had run down Main Street and under the Quilt Lady, the proof that the vein had gone dry over a hundred years ago was in the archives at Barstow.

Not that Drew intended to tell him. He'd let the SOB learn the hard way. But he didn't intend to stand quietly aside and let Andrews court Leslie.

"I used to be a champion professional boxer," Andrews threatened. "You might want to reconsider."

"Not a chance." Drew answered. "I boxed a little myself. Just say where and when."

"You'll find out when I'm good and ready!" Andrews swallowed hard and stormed away.

It was a relief to stop inside Maddie's and inhale the odors of strong black coffee and fresh doughnuts. He needed to hear a friendly voice to still the growing apprehension that the day ahead wasn't going to be all fun and roses.

Maddie slid a plate with two freshly baked doughnuts toward him. "Have a cup of coffee," she said as she studied him. "Something riling you?"

"Yeah, you could say so," he replied, biting into a sugar doughnut. "Hope the coffee is good and strong this morning."

"Glad you like it that way. I don't know how to make any other kind," Maddie answered frankly. She filled a mug with thick, black coffee and handed it to him. "Cream and sugar?"

"No, black with a bite in it," Drew replied, staring angrily at the cup.

"Well, it's black, but not enough to bite you back. I have my reputation to consider," Maddie observed dryly. "What's up?"

"Keith Andrews," Drew muttered into his coffee.

"What's he up to?"

"He just boasted he intends to ask Leslie to marry him!"

"Wouldn't put it past him to try," Maddie answered with a frown. "What with the reward being offered and all."

"Where did you hear about the reward?" Drew searched his memory. Except for the one Andrews had kept, he was sure he'd managed to retrieve most of the flyers offering the reward.

The person with a loose mouth had to be the man who printed them for the kids and took their five bucks for his trouble—Strawberry.

Drew added him to the growing list of men he intended to educate about respecting a woman—one way or another. He'd see that they left Leslie and her boys alone before he moved on. At the rate the list was growing, it didn't look as if he'd be leaving any time soon.

"You might say that word has gotten around about the reward," Maddie answered. "Although how those kids could come up with any money beats me."

Her look plainly told him she didn't intend to say anything further.

"You're not going to tell me, are you?"

"No way. I'm trying to save you from yourself. Judging from the way you looked when you came in here, someone could get himself killed." She studied him with a bemused look. "Don't know why, but I like you, McClain. I'd hate to see you get into real trouble before you leave for greener pastures."

"Who said I was leaving?" He was tired of being

reminded he hadn't intended to stay in Calico. It was his business and no one else's, not even Maddie's.

"You did. I heard you myself the other day—right over at the table over there. In fact, you and Leslie were hollering at each other so loud, half the town must have heard you tell her you weren't going to hang around after Hullabaloo."

Maddie was right. He recalled his first meeting with Leslie when she'd threatened to use her office to force him to baby-sit her boys. He recalled his bitter answer. He'd told Leslie off loud enough to be heard all the way to Vegas, let alone throughout Calico.

But that was before he'd gotten to know Leslie. Before he'd realized what drove her to be the best damned mayor and mother in California. And before he found the woman under that cool exterior.

"Want to change your mind about leaving?" Maddie's question shook him.

Drew stared into his cup of coffee. "To tell the truth, I haven't given it much thought until now." Not before he found out whether he was really welcome in Leslie's life.

"Didn't think so." She sighed. "Traveling men like you and Ben can't stay in one place for long."

"I thought you liked Ben."

"Sure do, but a fat lot of good it'll do me," she said wistfully. "From what he's told me, Ben's been on the road since he was knee-high to a grasshopper. Don't figure he's going to change now."

"I don't know about that, Maddie." Drew polished off the last of his doughnut, wiped crumbs off his fingers and stood to leave. "You could be wrong. Ben seems to be real taken with you."

"Just like you're taken with Leslie?"

Drew set his coffee cup back on the counter. He liked Maddie, liked her well enough to be sorry Ben Rubard had shown up to make her yearn for something she couldn't have. As for Leslie, Maddie had him there. Would he be a rotter if he left Leslie the way Ben was going to leave Maddie?

"Maybe so," he answered truthfully. Was his attraction to Leslie that obvious?

The life he'd known was fading fast. Calico and its world was closing in on him.

He'd been looking for something and someone special for more than ten long, empty years. Could they possibly be waiting for him here in Calico?

"Things aren't always what they seem to be on the surface, Maddie," he said as he waved goodbye.

He glanced at his watch. It was time to pick up Leslie and take her to the rodeo. Time enough to ponder the future later. After he had a chance to sound out how Leslie felt about him.

When he reached the Quilt Lady, Leslie was locking the door behind her and the kids were gone. So much for a chance to come to an understanding before it was too late. Or to tell her about the bet as his sixth sense was urging him to do.

"Sure you have to leave now?" he asked as he took the steps two at a time.

Leslie regarded him with a whimsical smile. "No, but the boys are waiting for me."

"Not as long as *I've* been waiting for you," he began, before he got a good look at her.

Today she was outfitted in western jeans and a blue T-shirt with a Make This Year A Hullabaloo logo printed on the front. Stylish western boots were on her feet. Her hair was newly washed and tightly braided. She wore a sun visor that barely concealed the teasing look in her emerald-green eyes.

Mayor Leslie Chambers was gone. A smiling, flirtatious woman dressed in tight-fitting jeans and a shirt that hugged the lovely womanly body he'd spent last night exploring had taken her place. She looked as if she'd stepped out of a contemporary magazine cover, as sassy as any model and just as beautiful.

"Don't you like the outfit?" she asked when she noticed the way his eyes widened.

"You look great—like a different woman," he replied. When her smile began to fade, he backtracked. "Not that I didn't like the woman you were before. In fact, I like any way you come packaged."

She was a fascinating bundle of contradictions. First, she'd been a mayor, all business and determined to be in control. Last night she'd turned into the warm and willing woman of his dreams. Today, she was a woman of the nineties: frank and not ashamed to show off her sensuality.

He wanted to take her in his arms and show her just how much he admired and, yes, desired every inch of her. Too bad they were in clear sight of the tourists arriving for today's celebration. He couldn't bring himself to add fuel to the fire swirling around them in the form of a bet. A bet that was sure to end his new relationship with Leslie if she heard of it.

Instead, he reached out to finger an auburn tendril that had escaped from her braid. A pleasing scent of perfume clung to her. There was a new softness to her, an inner glow shining through her eyes.

The gentle summer breeze brought with it the sounds of growing revelry. In the distance, he heard the shouts of the rodeo getting under way. He had the feeling time was running out for a quiet exchange of the entire truth between Leslie and himself.

And before Andrews kept his promise to tell Leslie a pack of lies. Lies that might send Drew on his way before he had a chance to tell her the story of the bet as he knew it.

And, above all, that somehow he had fallen in love with her.

It was now or maybe never.

"You don't suppose we could go on inside for a few minutes, do you?" His heart beat wildly in his chest while he waited for her answer.

Leslie put a hand on his arm. "Is there something wrong?"

"No. It's only that I have so much more to tell you," he said quietly.

Their eyes met. He saw her soften as she gazed at the longing he knew smoldered in his eyes.

She unlocked the door to the shop. "I guess you'd better come inside where it's a little more private."

"Leslie," he began once they were inside the shop. "There are some things I left unsaid last night. Things I have to tell you."

''Tell me later,'' she murmured as she went into his waiting arms.

He seized her lips with his and kissed her deeply again and again as if he would never let her go. Kiss for kiss, taste for taste, his desperation that he might lose her drove him on. He wanted nothing more than to take her upstairs, where they could lose themselves in a private world of their own making.

He pulled back when he realized Leslie was gazing at him in wonder. He knew that if he continued to press her against his rampant desire, they would be upstairs in minutes. But, somewhere in the back of his mind, common sense was trying to be heard.

''You're sure nothing's wrong?''

''No, nothing is wrong,'' he groaned. ''It's just that there are a couple of things I should have told you last night. The trouble is,'' he said against the vein that beat madly in her throat, ''when I'm holding you like this I find it hard to remember just what they were.''

Leslie laughed breathlessly. ''Then they can't be that important, can they? Just hold me for a minute. You can explain later.''

Drew breathed deeply, willing his body to cool. He'd waited all his adult life for this woman, if he had to wait a few more hours, he would.

He ran a finger across her reddened lips, kissed her lightly on her forehead. ''You're right. The last thing you need is more gossip. I wouldn't want to be the cause of any more talk than there's already been.''

Leslie gazed at him. ''Don't worry,'' she said. ''I refuse to let gossip bother me now. I promise we'll have a chance to talk later,'' she added. ''Today I intend to be Leslie Chambers. I want to play tourist and enjoy the rodeo.''

He grinned and gestured to his costume. "Do I still have to look like Wyatt Earp?"

"Of course," she answered primly. "You *are* the law around here."

She eyed his gun belt and holster dubiously. "Although I'm not sure you need to wear a gun. You haven't worn one before."

"Things have changed," he answered. "But don't worry, it's not loaded. It's mostly for show. At least, it'll intimidate some of the more boisterous guests."

What she didn't know wouldn't hurt her, Drew decided. And he intended to keep it that way.

No matter what.

"MOM! MR. MCCLAIN!"

Tim hurled himself at his mother. "Guess what Mr. Rubard let me do?"

Leslie wrinkled her nose, kissed him quickly and held him at arm's length. She glanced at Drew with a wry expression. "I'm sure I know, but you can tell me about it later after you get cleaned up."

Tim couldn't wait. "He let me and Jeremy exercise some of the horses after we helped clean up the stables! To warm them up for later, he said. And next, if you say it's okay, he's going to show us how to ride."

Leslie smiled. "I thought you already knew how to ride."

"Real riding! And to do tricks on the back of a horse!"

Leslie paled. She looked to Drew for help.

"I don't think you understood Ben," he said. "Trick riding is for experienced cowboys. Not for kids your age."

"I'm going to be a cowboy when I grow up," Tim insisted. "I got to start learning how right now!"

Drew knew all too well that childish dreams sometimes came true. And it was not always for the best. Since the boys were being raised in a western town without a decent male role model—what else could Leslie expect?

He caught a glimpse of Andrews hovering in the background. Camera in hand, he was in the process of taking pictures of the tourists to sell later. To make sure Andrews didn't get a chance at Leslie, Drew intended to stick to her like glue for the rest of the day.

"Why don't you fellows find yourselves a seat in the grandstand and try to stay out of trouble?"

"Ben said we could sit with the other cowboys, Mr. McClain!" Tim protested. "Jeremy's already there waiting for me."

"I don't think so," Leslie spoke up.

"Why not!"

"Because you're not a cowboy yet. Now, go and get your brother and bring him back here."

"Ah, Mom!"

"Listen to your mother, you can visit with Ben later." Drew's admonition sent Tim down to the corral.

"Thanks," Leslie said with a grateful smile. "I'm going to find us seats in the grandstand. Are you coming along?"

"Soon," Drew replied. He wanted to stay beside her, but he couldn't. He'd seen Andrews lose himself in the crowd—he had to find him and warn him away from Leslie.

Down below, Ben waved to him to join him. He waved back. From Ben's expression, something was on the man's mind.

"I'll be back as soon as I can. Take care of yourself."

Leslie's expression turned quizzical; she glanced at his holster. "Are you expecting trouble?"

"Not if I can help it," he muttered as he walked away.

He wanted to hold her, whisper the whole story of what was troubling him in her ear—and Andrews *was* trouble. But, unless he had time to fully explain himself, maybe it was better just to keep on praying for now.

"What's up, Ben?"

His friend looked uncomfortable. He folded his arms and leaned against a fence rail. "It's about Madelyn."

"Who's Madelyn?"

"I mean, Maddie." Ben's Adam's apple moved as he swallowed his embarrassment.

The idea of down-to-earth Maddie confiding her hidden given name to Ben, a virtual stranger, seemed downright funny. Until he saw the serious expression on Ben's face. This was obviously no laughing matter.

"So what about Maddie?"

Ben leaned over, picked up a length of straw and stuck it between his teeth. "You might say I'm kinda gone on her. And her cooking."

"So, what's the problem?"

"I think she's fixing to ask me to give up the rodeo and stick around here."

"Sounds good to me. How do you feel about that?"

"Can't. Still got the traveling fever." Ben answered as if it explained everything.

Drew nodded sympathetically. "I know what you mean. I used to have it myself."

Ben eyed him for a moment, then glanced up at the grandstand. "It's too late for me, but you're not too old to change. 'Specially since you have the mayor and her kids waiting for you."

"Come on, Ben." Drew laughed. "Did Maddie send you to talk to me?"

"Sort of. But it didn't take much for me to see how the two of you look at each other."

Drew froze. If it had become that obvious to Ben, no wonder Andrews had decided it was time to take action.

"I'll think about it," he answered, anxious to get back to Leslie's side. "How about you and Maddie?"

"Hell, I'm too old for wedding bells." Ben grinned. "But I did promise to come to dinner whenever I get close enough."

Drew was ready to bank on the drawing power of Maddie and her cooking.

But Ben might be right at that. Drew wasn't too old to change. As he noted the wistful look that came over the rodeo manager's face, Drew realized he didn't want to spend the rest of his life looking back at lost opportunity like Ben.

It struck him that what he'd been searching for was right here in Calico. A place to call his own, a woman to love and, yes, even a family. He looked up at the clear blue sky, half expecting to see a rainbow. For sure as shooting, the pot of gold was right under his nose. All he had to do was to reach for it.

Leslie and the kids were seated almost all the way to the top of the grandstand. He took the steps two at a time.

Only to find Andrews whispering in her ear.

Chapter Twelve

The way Andrews was looking at Leslie told Drew that this time he was going to have to punch Andrews out. The feeling in his gut warned him the guy was about to make good his threat to tell Leslie that Drew had boasted no woman was going to tame him. And that Drew had been so sure that *he* was going to be the one to tame Leslie, Drew had offered to take bets on it.

Since his relationship with Leslie was so new, there was a chance she might actually believe the bastard.

Drew's blood turned cold, his heart into a block of ice. He could almost hear the sound of it harden and crack. Had the realization he loved Leslie and that his wandering days were over come too late?

Muttering curses under his breath, he made the remaining stairs of the stadium bleachers in triple time. If Andrews was going to play dirty, Drew intended to be there to defend himself.

"Would you do me the honor of having dinner with me tonight?" he heard Andrews ask Leslie.

"The lady is taken," Drew growled, struggling to catch his breath. "Find yourself another pigeon!"

"Who asked you?" Andrews blustered. "I'm inviting Leslie, not you. Why don't you let the lady speak for herself?''

''She's already told you before she's not interested,'' Drew retorted. ''What does it take to get the message across?'' He was well aware that once Andrews got Leslie alone, he'd play on her sympathy.

''There's nothing you can do to stop me,'' Andrews replied. ''I have just as much right to Leslie as you do! Maybe more!''

Leslie gasped. Motioning the fascinated boys to stay behind her, she stepped between Drew and Keith Andrews. ''That's enough testosterone out of both of you. I've told you both before I will not tolerate a debate on whom I belong to! I belong to myself. As for accepting a date, I can make up my own mind.''

With her mayoral mask back in place, she glared at the photographer. ''You're out of line, Mr. Andrews. I've already told you I'm not interested.''

She raked Drew with an angry gaze. ''And as for you, what gives you the right to choose whom I can date?''

''You're right,'' he answered, cursing himself for putting them in this position. Seeing her anger, he realized maybe he *had* read too much into their night together. But, loving aside, dammit, someone had to look out for her.

He should have told her before now he'd decided to give up his wandering. And that he had realized he loved her. He ached to tell her he thought last night gave him the right to protect her, to keep her safe from scum like Andrews.

Clearly agitated, Leslie took off her sun visor and

fanned herself with it. A glance at her shining braided hair reminded him he'd wondered if Leslie had given of herself completely to him last night. If not, then he *didn't* have the right to keep her from seeing another man.

Damn! If only Andrews hadn't decided on a public challenge!

Obviously sensing this wasn't the right time or place to stake a claim to Leslie, Andrews faded into the background—to Drew's relief.

While most of the spectators couldn't possibly know Leslie was Calico's mayor, she still had her pride and her dignity to preserve. He couldn't argue with her; he couldn't shame her that way. He'd have to take a chance their night together had meant as much to her as it had to him and try again later.

Drew could see the fright on Jeremy's and Tim's faces, saw them reach for their mother's hands. Heads began to turn in their direction. It wouldn't take much more to cause a scene he'd regret.

Before he left, Drew squeezed the boys' shoulders in passing to reassure them everything was going to be okay.

Not that he was sure yet everything *would* be okay, he mused as he headed back uptown. Andrews could offer Leslie marriage and stability of a sort. Maybe that *was* something Leslie wanted. As for himself, even if he told her he loved her and asked her to marry him, what did he have to offer her except himself?

Old doubts surfaced. After a lifetime of wandering, he didn't have much to give Leslie beyond his love and devotion. And his willingness to pledge every ounce of strength in him to make her happy.

HE WAS BACK in the jailhouse thinking he ought to gather up his few belongings in case Andrews had told his dirty lies and Leslie believed them. He couldn't face another put-down.

He paced the floor waiting for the other shoe to drop. Then he halted in mid-stride. Hell, no! He was no quitter. He wasn't going to hang around the jail any longer before he straightened out a few misunderstandings, and Keith Andrews to boot!

A redheaded bundle of fury stormed in before he could make his plans. Leslie looked disheveled enough to have come through a storm—and maybe she had. An emotional one, anyway.

"How could you have started a bet like that? How could you have boasted that you intended to tame me?" Eyes blazing with anger, Leslie shook a small fist under his nose. "You, of all people!"

Drew knew enough to let her wind down before he took her on. The truth was on his side, if he could only get her to calm down long enough so she could hear it.

"It would help if you let me in on what I'm supposed to have done," he said when she paused to catch her breath. He knew all right—Andrews had spread his venom as promised, but he wanted to know how far the man had gone.

"Andrews told me all about the bet!" Her green eyes flashed, her face was crimson with her anger. "How could you stoop so low? How could you have made that kind of bet behind my back and then make love to me? Was it to win the bet?''

So, she *had* been affected by their making love. Looking at her now, Lord, how he wanted her again!

''Now wait a minute,'' he cut in. ''He told you a pack of lies!''

''Are you saying you didn't boast you could melt me down, Calico's ice lady?'' she sputtered angrily. ''That you could tame me before I could tame you?''

''There's a bet like that going around, all right, but I didn't make it,'' he answered. ''And if you give me a few minutes, I'll tell you the story as far as I know it.''

''Go ahead,'' she challenged. She glanced at her wristwatch. ''You have just five minutes before I'm going to have you run out of town!''

''Five minutes? Is that all I'm worth to you?''

''Under the circumstances,'' she glowered, ''that's probably more than enough.''

He sucked in his breath and started in. ''From the way I understand it, a few of the men heard our argument the first day we met for coffee at Maddie's. One of them, and I don't know who exactly, decided to make some easy money and started a betting pool on who would tame who first.''

Leslie shook her head and glared at him. ''That's not the way I heard the story!''

''I'm sure it wasn't, especially if Andrews told it to you! Sorry, but that's the way the betting got started. I didn't even hear about the bet until I stumbled on it later.''

''Later? How? And why didn't you tell me?''

Drew's heart sank. He couldn't tell her about the kids' flyers advertising a reward for a man to marry their mother. Not without making her feel even more exposed. Plus get the kids in trouble they would never be allowed to forget. Sure, she'd overheard the boys plotting to try to figure out a way to get her married, she'd told him so herself. But to have actually advertised for a dad, and make her the butt of jokes? He couldn't bring himself to tell her that. Besides, the kids were too young to have realized the possible outcome. Or that it might break their mother's heart.

He raised his right hand. "I swear to you with everything in me I didn't dream up the betting. You have to trust I'm telling you the truth. If you don't believe me, ask anyone—except Andrews."

He could see Leslie considering his suggestion. She'd already told him she'd held on to her distrust of men for years before she'd decided Drew was the one man different than the rest of the men she knew. She must have known *he* didn't have to put a woman down in order to feel like a real man.

The least she could do was give him a chance to tell his side of the story.

"All right," she agreed. "I'm going to go out and grab the first man I can find. If he agrees you're telling the truth, I'll believe you." She turned on her heel and stormed out of the jail.

Drew knew he was in deep trouble as soon as he realized the only locals available were the shopkeepers—all the others were at the rodeo. And, damn it all, there was Alan Little and his pony rides. As dishonest a betting man as any in Calico.

Sure enough, Leslie was back in minutes dragging the protesting man behind her.

"I'm going to ask Alan if he knows who started the betting," she said. "He doesn't have an ax to grind. Go ahead, Alan."

When he met Drew's steady gaze, the livery stable owner seemed to shrink in his boots. Drew's heart sank. Little was a permanent resident of Calico and obviously knew where his bread and butter lay. It sure as hell wasn't with him.

"Well, you see, it was this way," Little began. "After the two of you got into an argument in Maddie's, betting which one of you was going to get the better of the other seemed like the natural thing to do."

Drew snorted.

"And?" Leslie prompted. "Who suggested the bet?"

Little shuffled his feet, glanced hopefully at the door and shook his head. "I don't remember."

"Was it me?" Drew asked quietly. When Little swallowed hard, Drew had his answer. The man was too frightened, too intimidated by Strawberry, Holliday and the rest of the men to give an honest answer.

"I don't remember," Little repeated. "Can I go now? I have kids waiting to ride my ponies."

Leslie let go of his arm. She waited until Little made good his escape before she turned on him. "Well, Mr. McClain, with you wearing that gun, it sounds as if Alan's too afraid of you to tell the truth. It doesn't matter—it looks as if I've gotten my answer."

If looks could kill, Drew figured he ought to be dead. He could have brought in Maddie as a character witness, but she had enough troubles of her own. Her income depended on the goodwill of the locals even more than Alan Little's.

The truth was, Drew *was* a stranger passing through. Under the circumstances, maybe he had no right to create problems for people who had to live and work together.

When Leslie shot him the look of a betrayed woman and turned on her heel to leave, the argument was over.

Drew gazed after her, too proud to ask her back and make her listen to reason. He'd leave town tonight, except that he was a man of his word. He was determined to finish out his verbal contract with the sheriff, come hell or high water.

Maybe Calico and its mayor weren't destined to become the treasure at the end of the rainbow, after all.

LESLIE HEADED for a quiet haven. Her quilt shop was a refuge where she'd stitched her dreams and hopes into the dozens of quilts she'd designed and sewn in the last three years. She could pour out her grief and hurt in small, even stitches. And try to put Drew McClain and his betrayal aside.

The apartment was empty. In her bedroom, the sight of her rumpled bed brought back images of herself and Drew joined in passion, lips to lips, heart to heart, skin to skin. And when she'd awakened this morning to find him stretched out on his side watching her.

Her uncertain smile had reignited his passion—time had flown by as though she was in a dream. She trembled, remembering the taste of him, the scent of him, the feel of his strong body against hers as he made love to her.

She could hardly bear to remain in the bedroom long enough to take off her jeans and T-shirt and change into costume. A glance into her mirror revealed the loose tendril of hair Drew had fingered that morning. With a sob, she tightened her braid and hardened her heart.

She had successfully kept a cold shell around her until Drew had managed to turn her thoughts in directions she'd almost forgotten. She should have known he was trouble as soon as he'd made love to her with his eyes. Instead, she'd plunged headlong into his arms.

She should have been smart enough to know she was being manipulated. How could she have let herself be betrayed by a man who clearly had an agenda of his own when he'd made love to her?

The answer sounded clear as a bell.

He'd made her fall in love with him.

HIDING BEHIND a water barrel that stood under the jail's lone window, Jeremy and Tim looked at each other.

"I'm scared," Tim announced. "What if Mr. McClain decides to leave? What if he doesn't want to be our dad?"

"Sure he does, only he doesn't know it yet." Jeremy stared off into the distance before he brightened. "Don't worry. I have another plan."

"Remember what Mr. McClain said about staying out of trouble!"

"No problem. This time, my idea can't miss," Jeremy assured his brother. "Come on."

He led the way to the miniature train that was about to leave on a tour of the Sweet Sue mine. "You go hide in the caboose. As soon as the train is out of the depot and the coast is clear, I'll jump on."

"I don't want to see an old silver mine," Tim protested. "I want to go talk to Mr. McClain. Maybe I can get him to change his mind about leaving."

"How are you going to do that? Besides, we've already tried."

"I could tell him how much we both love him and how much we want a dad," Tim said wistfully.

"He already knows that, stupid. It's Mom we have to convince." Jeremy threw his arm across his brother's shoulders and gave him a sympathetic hug. "Maddie's headed this way. If she sees us, she's gonna know we're up to something. Better go on and get in the caboose as soon as no one's looking."

"WHAT'S BEEN GOING ON in here?" Maddie demanded as she blew into the jail like a tornado.

"Not much." Drew forced a grin. Bless her heart, Maddie did nothing halfway. Whether it was cooking up the best meal in San Bernardino County or straightening him out.

"No?" She planted her hands on her hips and eyed him curiously. "I saw Leslie drag Alan inside here. When he hightailed out, it was like the devil was chasing him. Then I see Leslie storming out of here. I called to her, but she didn't stop."

Drew shrugged philosophically. Having Maddie's Last Chance Café across the street didn't give him much of an opportunity to keep anything from the lady dragon. Not that he had anything to hide, but he wasn't in the mood for another lecture.

"Just a small difference of opinion," he answered. "It'll pass."

"No way!" she countered. "Too bad I had to wait until my customer was gone before I could lock up and come over. If I'd have known all he wanted was a dozen doughnuts, I would have put out my Closed sign ten minutes ago."

She regarded Drew closely, too closely, in his opinion. He clamped his lips shut and eyed her back.

"Don't want to talk?"

"No more than you did when I questioned you before," he replied.

"That's because it's a wise man who knows when to keep his mouth shut," Maddie answered. "But somehow I don't think that's true this time."

They studied each other, neither one willing to give an inch.

"Since Alan Little is involved, something tells me your argument involves the bet. And I'm not leaving until you tell me about it," Maddie announced. She dropped into the chair facing the desk. "Am I right?"

"Maybe."

"No maybes about it," she snapped. "After last night, it's probably the *only* thing that could have riled her up so."

Drew shrugged.

"Why didn't you ask me to come over? I could have straightened Leslie out."

"You? *Now* you're willing to talk?"

"Well, there's a time and place for everything." She grinned. "Besides, there's that bet."

Drew leaned across the desk. "Did it ever occur to you that if *I* tamed Leslie, you and the rest of the ladies would lose?"

"Yeah," she admitted. "But sometimes a bet is worth losing. Besides, that was before I got to know you."

"What made you change your mind?"

"I decided you're the best thing that's happened to Leslie in a long time. And as for the rest of the town, it's about time Calico got itself a permanent, full-time sheriff."

"Meaning me?"

"Meaning you. Who else?"

Drew shrugged. "I'm afraid you're a little late. Andrews has already gone to Leslie with the story that I was the one who dreamed up the bet and started the pool going. Right now, she wouldn't let Carrey hire me to clean out a henhouse."

"Hogwash! All of us know the truth, including me. And I'm just the one to tell it to her." She jumped out of her chair and made for the door.

"Hang on there, Maddie." Drew reached to stay her. "If Leslie couldn't bring herself to believe my side of the story, I don't want you to get involved. It's me she has to trust, and it doesn't look as if she's about to."

"Even after last night?"

Drew felt himself flush. "Even after last night," he repeated.

She studied him carefully. Apparently satisfied, she smiled. "You don't appear to me to be a hit-and-run sort of guy. Did you bother to tell Leslie you love her?''

''I'm afraid not, but I was going to tell her today. Along with a few other things. Only Andrews got in the way.''

''Have it your way,'' Maddie answered. She plastered her hands on the desk and locked her gaze with his. ''Just don't take too long to tell Leslie you've decided to give up wandering and that you love her. And don't forget to tell her you want to marry her!''

''I do?'' Drew grinned foolishly. Had he made himself that obvious? If Maddie had picked up on the way he felt about Leslie, why hadn't Leslie?

''You do,'' Maddie said flatly. ''Only like most men, having to admit you're wrong is a mite difficult. Most of you get there eventually, but you gotta do it the hard way.''

Drew grunted. ''Yeah, sure.''

''Want me to talk to Leslie for you?''

''No way. There are some things a man has to do for himself.''

''Then do it and don't waste any more time.'' Maddie straightened up and eyed him sternly.

TWO HOURS LATER, Drew saw Leslie rushing up the street from the rodeo grounds. She'd changed from her jeans and T-shirt into her costume. Her bonnet hung from her shoulders, her feet were flying. She looked upset as hell.

His heart sank. What more could Andrews have told her to rile her up this time?

She came to a stop in front of him. From the distraught expression on her face, he could have been any-one—certainly not the man who had held her in his arms and made passionate love to her less than twenty-four hours ago. Or even the man she'd disowned.

Hairs tingled at the nape of his neck. His sixth sense told him it wasn't himself or Andrews she had on her mind.

"Are the boys with you?" she cried. "I've been looking for them for the last hour! No one has seen them!"

"Hold on a minute," he cautioned. "Why don't you calm down and tell me everything you know."

He saw Leslie fight for control. He sensed something was different about the boys' latest escapade. She lifted her eyes to his searching gaze. It was clear she thought that if anyone could help her find the children, it was Drew.

"I left the boys with Ben after..." Her voice trailed off, her face colored. "You know, after..."

"Yeah, I know," Drew answered. "But now isn't the time to think about that. The boys are more im-portant. What happened after I left?"

"Jeremy and Tim looked so unhappy, I decided to let them sit with the cowboys down at the corral. I came back here intending to visit with the tourists for a while, but I couldn't get my mind off the expression on your face when you left." She looked embarrassed at her confession. "I decided to give you a chance to explain yourself, but things didn't go the way I hoped they would. Not after Alan didn't back you up."

Drew kept his face impassive, but his heart leapt in his chest at the word "hope." She *had* cared for him, but he'd been too full of hurt male pride to insist she listen to him then and there as he should have. But having Andrews close enough to hear his explanations had been more than he could handle.

"What happened then?"

"I went back to the shop. I became so involved in piecing a new quilt, I didn't notice how much time was going by. When it got near to dinner time, I decided to bring the boys home. They weren't there. Ben said they'd been gone for hours."

Drew ached to wipe away the tears that had gathered at the corners of her eyes. To hold her against him, assure her he'd find the boys and everything would turn out all right. Until he realized they'd get further if he kept his mind clear and his actions objective.

Showing her how much he loved her would have to wait.

"Have you asked around to see if anyone noticed the kids this afternoon?"

"Some," she replied, wiping her tears away with an endearing gesture that reminded him of Tim. "I guess I panicked when I turned up empty. That's when I came looking for you."

"You did the right thing," Drew answered, hopeful again, since she'd turned to him for help. He looked around the town teeming with tourists, sidewalk vendors and fortune-hunters.

There were plenty of places for the kids to hide, but this couldn't just be a game of hide-and-seek. In addition to the rodeo and games, there was too much going on for the boys to want to miss out.

"I'm going to start up one end of the street and

down the other, ask if anyone has seen the boys and pass the word to send the kids home if they see them. Why don't you go on into the jailhouse and wait for me?''

He changed his mind when he saw Leslie appeared to be too frightened to be left alone. ''Would you feel better if you waited at Maddie's?''

''No,'' she answered. ''I think I'll feel better if you'll let me go with you.''

His heart went out to Leslie. How could he insist she remain behind not knowing if her boys were safe?

He nodded. This time Leslie was asking him, not telling him. Grateful, he hoped it meant she believed and trusted him, after all.

Leslie followed him from shop to shop and helped question anyone who might know her boys. When questions failed to turn up any information, a dread premonition filled her. What if Jeremy and Tim had outdone themselves this time? What if they'd never be found alive?

She moaned. Drew reached for her hand and clasped it in his own. He stroked the back of her wrist gently until she looked up into his eyes. ''We're going to find them,'' he told her softly, ''and that's a promise!''

In spite of her fears, Leslie found herself believing Drew. Why hadn't she realized before that he'd kept every promise he'd made to her, from the very first day they'd met? And why hadn't she listened when Tim and Jeremy had tried to tell her how much they liked Drew and wanted her to like him too? Maybe none of this would have happened if she had. When she found her boys, she vowed, she'd try harder to be more patient.

In the few days he'd been the law in Calico, Drew had earned her respect and that of most of Calico's citizens. At least, until the bet had surfaced. Why hadn't she trusted him long enough to believe he'd told her the truth?

She knew why, and hated herself for knowing. She'd been afraid to yield all of herself, to make herself vulnerable. Afraid one morning she'd wake up to find him gone, she'd held part of herself back. She'd been trying to keep herself from having her heart broken again.

WHEN NO NEWS about the boys turned up, Drew headed for the firehouse with Leslie.

"I want you to call out the search-and-rescue team," he told her. "As the mayor, you're probably the only one who can."

She felt herself pale. "You don't think the boys have fallen down one of the mines, do you?"

"No," he said shortly. "But we have to start somewhere. I'm sure the team knows the mines around here better than anyone else."

Leslie hurried into the firehouse office and spoke to the man on watch. Seconds later, a siren screamed into the air and reverberated against the hills.

"The volunteer firemen will be here as soon as they hear the siren," she told Drew. Stark terror filled her eyes.

"Don't worry," Drew said. He smiled his reassurance. "I understand you have a crackerjack search-and-rescue team. Between us, we're bound to find the boys.''

He cornered a teenage boy who had been attracted by the commotion.

''What's your name, son?''

''Lucas Harding, Mr. McClain. What's going on?''

''Never mind, I'll tell you later. Right now, I want you to do an errand for me. Okay?'' The boy nodded eagerly. ''Run down to the rodeo and ask to speak to Ben Rubard. Tell him to bring some of his boys and their horses here pronto.''

''Got it!''

''What good can Ben do?'' Leslie asked fearfully as the boy raced off. ''He's pretty much a stranger around here.''

''You'll see,'' he assured her. ''We're going to take the search one step at a time.''

Volunteer firemen poured out of the shops and into the street. ''What's going on, McClain?''

''I need the search-and-rescue team. Are any of you here?''

Eight men stepped forward.

''Good. All of you know the Chambers boys?'' Heads nodded.

''You don't mean to say those kids have been at it again, do you?'' Doc Parsons elbowed his way to the front of the crowd. ''I thought you straightened out the Chambers family?''

He looked pointedly at Leslie.

''Look here, Doc!'' Maddie thundered. ''This is no time to look for any more problems than the one we've got. I say we keep our minds on finding the kids.'' She looked belatedly at Drew. "They *are* lost, aren't they?"

"Maybe, maybe not," Drew answered. He waited until Ben and a few of his mounted men rode up.

"Ben, do you suppose you and your men could fan out across the hills and into the desert before it gets dark? Jeremy and Tim may be somewhere out there."

Ben nodded to Maddie, gave Leslie a reassuring smile and summoned his riders. "Sure thing. Come on, boys. Let's go find the kids!"

Maddie beamed with pride as the horses raced out of town in a cloud of dust.

"As for you men on the team," Drew went on, "I'd like you to think about the mines around here. Which are the most likely ones the boys could have gotten into?"

Alan Little spoke up. "Now that you mention it, I did see the two of them hanging around the railroad a few hours back."

"Why haven't you said something before now?" Leslie cried. "You knew the boys were missing!"

The man looked affronted. "Because I was busy selling tickets for pony rides, that's why!"

Before Leslie could start for the livery stable owner, Drew grabbed her, pulled her against his chest and put his arms around her. He didn't give a damn about what anyone thought of the intimate gesture or if his actions might be construed as a show of ownership. Alan Little wasn't worth fighting over and they were losing time.

"If the kids got aboard the train's last run, it's damned sure they're in the Sweet Sue," Clement O'Reilly, the train's engineer, announced.

"Okay! Let's get a move on," Drew answered.

Grumbling about the poor timing of the Chambers boys' latest caper, the rescue team gathered their equipment and headed for the train.

Chapter Thirteen

Leslie huddled close to Drew as the miniature train with its open cars chugged slowly through the entrance of the Sweet Sue mine. The only light came from the train's headlamp and the flashlights held by Drew and the rescue crew. To add to his sense of foreboding, the dancing lights revealed boarded-up openings to secondary tunnels. There was no sign of the boys, nothing to indicate they'd been here or wandered off the main track.

Even the other rescuers seemed to be awed by the deep silence and the darkness where the slightest whisper seemed to have an ominous echo.

To signal the missing boys, O'Reilly periodically pulled on the train's whistle. There was only the sound of the whistle's echo, no answering shouts or calls for help. The cold air and the eerie silence emphasized the gravity of the situation. Drew couldn't remember ever feeling so inadequate.

He felt Leslie shudder. He put his free arm around her, pulled her close and whispered words of comfort.

Soon, in the glare of the flashlight, he spotted a

boarded-up opening. A few of the weathered boards had been broken off and lay in the dirt.

"Stop! I think I see something!" he called. As soon as the train ground to a halt, he vaulted out of the open car, sprinted back to the opening and began to pull off the remaining boards. "Look, there's footprints in the dirt. The boys are somewhere in there. I'm going in."

"Better let us come with you," Doc Parsons advised. "If the tunnel was boarded up, it means it's not safe to go in. You don't know what you're going to find in there. At the rate the roofs of these old tunnels collapse, you'd think they'd been shored up with spit."

Drew's blood ran cold. "Maybe you'd better wait out here, Leslie." When she shook her head, he uttered a prayer for the boys' safety and started into the opening.

"Better lower your voices. Sounds can trigger a cave-in," Lucas Miller, the head of the search team, cautioned. "No use asking for trouble."

Drew nodded. "Maybe we ought to go in one at a time? I'll go first."

"You know anything about mines?" Miller inquired.

"No, but if the boys are hiding, they might show themselves faster if they see me."

"You could be right, it's worth a try." Miller eyed him thoughtfully. "Okay, you can lead the way but I'll be right behind you. The rest of you fellows follow us at two-minute intervals. Sure you want to go in there, Leslie?"

The look on her face stopped him. "Okay, you can

follow me. In case there's a cave-in, there'll be some-one to go for help.''

Cave-in? Go for help? Drew shuddered. Things were going from bad to worse. If he *did* manage to get the kids out of this stupid stunt unharmed, he intended to see to it they walked the straight and narrow from now on. No matter if it took him the rest of his life.

His face hidden by the darkness, he had to smile. For a man who hadn't planned on remaining in Calico for more than a few days, he was making plans well into the future. And for two children he couldn't call his own. Still, if he did ask Leslie to marry him, the kids would come as part of the package.

He was beginning to think there might be a possi-bility the boys had accomplished their mission to find a dad.

"Tim? Jeremy?" he called in a loud whisper. "It's me, Drew. Come on out."

"Hell, if those two kids are hiding, they aren't going to give in that easily," O'Reilly remarked quietly as Leslie murmured a protest. "We ought to know—this isn't the first time we've had to pull them out of scrapes."

"Anything as bad as this one?" Drew asked. He continued to walk carefully, shining his flashlight on the floor.

"No, can't say that they were," O'Reilly answered under his breath. "But I guess it was a matter of time until they thought up this stunt. They've tried every-thing else."

Particles of soil and small clouds of dust trickled down on them as Drew carefully examined the ground ahead of him. It must have been years since anyone had come through this tunnel. Suddenly, O'Reilly bumped into him.

Drew staggered. "Hold up a minute, I've dropped my light." He went down on his knees to grope for his flashlight. When he rose to his feet, he noticed an opening in the wall.

He shone the flashlight into the narrow cave. Clasped in each other's arms for comfort, Jeremy and Tim were fast asleep. He straightened, raised his arm and clicked the flashlight on and off three times in the prearranged signal that the boys had been found.

He realized they'd made enough noise to disturb the dirt ceiling of the tunnel when a dribble of sandy soil fell on him. A sense of urgency filled him as he motioned the others to stay back. "Come on, Tim, Jeremy, wake up," he whispered. "I've come to take you home."

Tim was the first to awaken. When he saw Drew staring at him, he shook his brother awake. He heard his mother's voice call his name. "Mom?"

"You can talk to your mother later. Let's get moving."

"I'm glad you found us," Tim said nervously while he and Jeremy inched their way out of the cave. "Our flashlight died, and I don't like it in the dark."

Drew wasn't sure if he wanted to hug the boys or dust their rears. Maybe both. "We'll talk about it later. Right now, we've got to get you out of here."

At a sign from Drew, O'Reilly motioned to Leslie to back out of the tunnel, handed Jeremy to her and reached for Tim. Drew started to follow.

He could hear Leslie trying to comfort Tim when he heard the ominous sound of dry wooden boards give way above his head. Were they close enough to the tunnel's entrance to get out before the roof caved in?

He uttered a fervent prayer. He'd promised to return the boys to their mother, and he wasn't about to break that promise if he could help it. Dirt spilled over him as he scrambled the remaining distance out of the tunnel. Just as he reached the main track, he heard a loud thud behind him. They'd made it out in the nick of time.

When everyone reached the train, Doc Parsons gave the boys a cursory looking over. "They'll do," he said as he eyed them sternly, "but you might want to bring them by my office tomorrow so I can take a better look."

"Mom?" Tim spoke up. "I'm hungry."

Leslie laughed her relief and covered his smudged face with kisses. "We'll get something for you at Maddie's. I'm sure she'll find you something to eat."

Drew hid a relieved smile. In the midst of cold, darkness and danger, if all the kid could think of was food, he was okay.

He'd hoped to get the boys inside the café without a fuss, but his hopes died when he found a crowd waiting for them as the train pulled into the depot.

Before he had a chance to lead the boys across the street, the door to the café burst open and Maddie came charging out to gather the boys in her arms. Her eyes were shining but her cheeks were streaked with tears. Drew realized how much the boys meant to her—and yes, to him. He swallowed the lump in his throat.

"Mom? It's okay to punish me if you want," Jeremy said in a low voice. "But not Tim. It was all my fault."

"Not now," Leslie answered in a choked voice. "Maybe later." She forgot how angry she'd been when the boys turned up missing. Or the last agonizing hours when she'd imagined the terrible things that could have happened to them. She only knew it felt wonderful to have her children in her arms again. She held the boys to her and never wanted to let them go.

"Promise me you won't run away again," she told them as she smoothed their hair. "If you have something on your mind, tell me. We'll talk about it. Okay?"

"We tried, Mom," Tim said between sobs. "But you wouldn't listen."

"I will from now on," Leslie promised as she looked over their heads at Drew and muttered a thank-you. She hugged the boys to her again with a fierce gesture. "We'll all try harder. Just remember I love you."

Maddie cleared her throat. "Come on inside and bring the boys, Leslie. I have just the thing for a couple of boys who ought to be pretty hungry by now—a pot of hot vegetable soup and a plate of chocolate cookies." She gestured to the rescue team. "As for you men, I can have hot coffee here in a few minutes."

"Don't bother, Maddie," Doc Parsons answered wearily. "I don't know about the rest of the boys, but this has been a mite hard on me. Guess I'm getting too old for this sort of thing. I'm going up to bed." He turned to go. "Now remember, you boys—this is the last time I expect to have to come looking for you!"

The rest of the rescue team muttered their agreement and started for home.

Drew felt more alone than ever as he watched Leslie and the boys disappear into the Last Chance. Yet he hadn't come to Calico expecting gratitude. He'd done what Leslie had asked him to do, and he would have done it even if she hadn't asked him for help.

DREW WAS IN HIS OFFICE the next morning writing up a report on yesterday's rescue and a few other little items for Tom Carrey. He was careful to leave out any unnecessary, unflattering references to Leslie and her boys.

"Back again for another apology?" Drew asked, when Jeremy and Tim turned up in the jailhouse.

"Yeah. Mom said we had to apologize as part of our punishment," Jeremy answered.

"Sounds about right. An apology is a good place to start," Drew agreed, trying to remember if this was apology number three or four. "What's the rest of the punishment?"

"Mom hasn't told us yet," Tim announced. "She said she wants us first to think real hard about what we did."

Drew guessed that if anyone in the Chambers family needed time to think, it was Leslie. At the rate the boys got into trouble, she probably had run out of punishments to fit the crime by now.

"I'm getting tired of fishing you out of trouble," Drew announced. As much as he'd grown fond of the two, it was the simple truth. "This last stunt of yours was too close a call for me to slough it off as another prank. I'm past the point of excusing your stunts as a boys-will-be-boys thing. If Alan Little hadn't caught a glimpse of you at the railway depot earlier, you kids could still be lost in the Sweet Sue.

"And another thing," Drew frowned as he added, "you kids don't seem to keep your promises too well, do you?"

Jeremy hung his head and studied his boots. "Guess not."

"Do you mind telling me what you hoped to accomplish by hiding in an abandoned mine?"

"Well, it was like this," Jeremy answered slowly. "I was reading *Tom Sawyer*. When everyone thought Tom and Huck had drowned in the river, they felt sorry they'd been so mean to them." Drew's raised eyebrows hurried him on. "Afterward, everyone was nice to each other."

"And just what good would your disappearance have done for you?"

"With us out of the way, Mom would have been awfully grateful to you after you helped find us," Jeremy said earnestly. "I figured Mom and you would realize how much we like you and want you for our dad. And maybe even how much you both really liked each other."

"I see." In spite of the gravity of the boys' actions, Drew had trouble keeping a straight face. Jeremy's thought processes were convoluted enough to crack Drew's determination to make sure justice would be swift. "And did you intend to come back for your funeral if I couldn't find you?"

Jeremy blanched. Tim started to cry.

Drew let them dwell upon the possibility before he continued. "I think maybe you ought to read the book again. You're missing a lesson or two."

"But we knew you'd find us, Mr. McClain."

The kid was right. Drew would have moved heaven and earth and never quit until he'd found them. "But didn't you think I might not have gotten to you in time?"

He studied the crestfallen boys and tried to think of what he could do next to keep the kids in hand.

Two things were pretty clear. They needed more responsibilities to keep them busy and out of trouble, and a male role model to teach them right from wrong. He could take care of the first item. Too bad it didn't look as if the second part was going to be his territory.

He beckoned the boys over to the desk, opened a drawer and rummaged around.

"You first, Jeremy."

"What are you going to do to my brother, Mr. McClain?" Tim asked in a quavering voice when Drew's holster and gun came into view.

Drew swallowed a grin. "Don't worry, I'm not going to shoot you guys *this* time. The gun's not loaded." He thought for a quick second. "And it's off limits, you hear?"

The boys nodded.

Drew pinned a deputy sheriff's badge on Jeremy's shirt. Then it was Tim's turn. "I figure if you're on the right side of the law, you'll think twice before you pull any more stupid stunts like this. Fact is, I'm going to swear you both in as deputies."

"Real deputies?"

"Real deputies," Drew agreed. "At least, as long as I'm around here."

"Cool!" Tim whispered as he fingered his badge. His tears were gone. Even Jeremy looked impressed.

"Yeah, really cool," Drew echoed. "Now raise your right hands while I administer the oath of office." Two small arms shot up in the air.

"I promise never to run away again, to listen to my mother and to uphold the law." The boys eagerly repeated the oath. "Now see if you can keep the peace instead of disturbing it."

Tim fingered his shiny new badge and couldn't keep the smile off his face.

"What do we have to do now, Mr. McClain?"

"Stay out of trouble," Drew answered. "We've had more than enough around here lately," he added, piercing them with a significant look.

The firehouse bell began to toll as Drew spoke. "Don't move!" he commanded. "Stay right here and keep an eye on the jailhouse! I'm going out to find out what's gone wrong now. Thank heaven it's not the two of you this time."

He took a second look at the boys, paused long enough to lock the desk drawer for safety's sake and stalked out of the jail.

Black clouds were billowing out of the roof of Keith Andrews's photography shop when Drew pulled up. The fire truck and the rest of Calico's volunteer firemen were close behind. A bucket brigade quickly formed to douse any loose sparks that fell into the street.

Drew ordered bystanders to stay away from the building so the volunteer firemen could get a handle on the fire. He looked through the window to make certain no one was still inside the store. The fire seemed to be confined to a corner closet—the developing room? If so, the firemen would have the smoldering fire out in no time.

He spotted Andrews standing off to one side and clutching an armful of cameras. "What happened?"

"Someone set fire to my shop, that's what happened!"

"Sure it wasn't a short circuit somewhere? Maybe some of your chemicals heated up while you were working?"

"Hell, no! I know how to run my business." Still clearly agitated, Andrews peered around him. "I'm sure the fire started around the back of the building where the Chambers kids play. I wouldn't put it past them to have started it to get even with me." He pointed to Drew's badge. "As the so-called law around here, I expect you to get to the bottom of this."

Drew could think of several reasons why the kids would have wanted to get even with Andrews, but he kept his own counsel. "Get even with you? Why would they want to do that?"

"I told them to stay out of my way when I come calling on Leslie. Same as I told you to do!"

"That's a hell of way to court Leslie," Drew commented dryly. "You sure aren't going to make any points with her at that rate."

Leslie came up behind them in time to hear Andrews's complaint and Drew's answer. "What's this all about?" she demanded.

Andrews clamped his mouth shut. Drew grinned. The man was in deep enough trouble without his help.

"I distinctly heard you say my boys could have been behind this fire!" Leslie insisted. "You're absolutely wrong!"

"Come on, Leslie. With the way your kids keep getting into trouble, you know it's a possibility." Frank Holliday turned to the crowd for support. "Right, folks?"

"Wrong!" Drew answered loud enough for everyone in the vicinity to hear. "I can vouch for the boys. They've been back in the jailhouse with me. They couldn't possibly have started the fire."

Someone coughed into the sudden silence. Drew sensed the crowd believed him. From the way the fire was being put out so quickly, he also sensed that Andrews might have started the fire himself to collect insurance. The louse seemed too determined to acquire money one way or another.

"Guess you'd better check your wiring, Keith," Drew said. "And while you're at it, your insurance policy, too." He wasn't surprised to see a cunning look pass over the photographer's face.

Leslie shot Andrews an angry look. First, he'd been cozying up to her and now this! "You can forget taking me out to dinner, Mr. Andrews, and anything else, for that matter."

"But, Leslie, I only wanted to—"

"What makes you think I would be interested in you?"

As mayor, she'd been coolly polite to him and the other men in Calico when the occasion had required, and nothing had changed. Not that she'd thought much of Andrews to begin with, but this rush to judgement on her boys was the last straw. The man was a skunk.

She turned her back on Andrews and came face-to-face with Drew. "Are the boys really in the jail-house?" she whispered.

"Yes, as far as I know. And, in case you're asking, I'm not trying to cover up for them." He studied her anxious expression. Didn't she believe him about this either?

"I hope not," she answered shortly. "Please send them home. I'd go get them myself, but I had a customer in the shop about to buy a quilt." She scanned the curious crowd. "There she is! I can't let her get away. Now don't forget, tell the boys to come home right away."

"As soon as I'm finished with them," Drew answered. "And not before they understand enough is enough."

"Finished with them? What more could you possibly do than what you've tried already?"

Drew put his hands in his pockets before he gave in to the temptation to shake her until her auburn braid came undone. Fleetingly, the thought crossed his mind that he might never see Leslie with her hair down. "Look here, Ms. Mayor. Seems to me we've had this conversation before. You've made it pretty clear that you haven't any more use for me than the other men around here. But, for the record, I did keep an eye on the boys, but only because I wanted to. I still do. You asked me to straighten them out, and I'm not finished yet!"

She planted her hands on her hips and glared at him.

"A day or two more and I'll be out of here. After that, the boys are all yours," he went on. "Before then, I intend to make sure the kids understand their limits!"

"Just as long as you understand yours, Mr. Mc-Clain!"

"Oh, I understand my limits all right," he answered, returning her glare. "You've made them damned clear. Too bad you keep changing the boundary lines." He took a deep breath and clamped his lips shut. There were too many curious people listening to the latest in the string of endless arguments he seemed to have with Leslie. The only good thing about this argument was that it left the pool high and dry without an answer to the bet. As far as he was concerned, neither one of them had been tamed.

"If you'll pardon me," he added, wishing he hadn't left his hat back at the jail so he could tip down the brim to hide his growing frustration. "I think this is where I came in." He turned on his heel and strode back to the jailhouse.

Leslie remained rooted to the spot. Filled with a longing to rush after him and apologize for her latest fit of temper, she gazed after Drew. She hadn't intended to get into another shouting match with him, but her nerves had gotten the better of her. Why did she continue to bait him when what she really wanted was to have him take her in his arms and make love to her again?

From the moment she'd asked him to spend the night with her, she'd known they were at a crossroads. Instead of placing herself and their future in his hands as she should have done, she'd actually listened to Keith Andrews's gossip. It hadn't taken her long to realize Andrews had his own agenda and it had nothing to do with his being in love with her. Why hadn't she gone after Drew right away and let him explain himself and believe him?

What had made her back away from him just when she'd sensed he was the verge of telling her he loved her? And just when she was about to tell him she loved him?

Part of the answer was her pride. The other part was she'd been a coward, afraid to let herself believe a man like Drew would want her enough to give up his wandering ways for a life like hers.

"DREW! COME ON HERE for a minute!" Maddie called when Drew came back. "Ben's inside and wants to say goodbye before he leaves."

Grateful for the interruption, Drew gritted his teeth and crossed the street to the café. In his frustration, if he'd gone back to the jail he'd more than likely have vented his feeling on the boys.

What he ached to do was to go back, find Leslie and make her listen. Tell her he loved her. Tell her how sorry he was that they were ending up like this. But Ben was waiting.

"Leaving so soon?" he asked his friend. "I kind of thought you'd be sticking around a while longer."

"Been in the saddle too long to get off now," Ben replied with a sidelong glance at Maddie. "But I'll be seeing you around from time to time."

Drew ignored the question on Maddie's face. It was

bad enough to know he'd be saying goodbye himself in a day or two without talking about it. Too bad her predictions about Leslie and him getting together hadn't come true.

He shook hands with Ben. "Good luck. I'll keep an eye out for you."

When he finally got back to the jailhouse, he found Jeremy and Tim seated where he'd left them an hour ago. They eyed him warily.

"Everything okay?" he asked. When they didn't answer, he took off his badge and threw it on the desk.

"Guess the two of you can go on home now. Your mother is looking for you."

Drew frowned when the kids remained rooted in their seats. They'd been up to something or his name wasn't Drew McClain.

"Didn't you kids hear me? I said you can go home now. Your mother is looking for you."

"Yeah, we know," Tim answered.

Drew was baffled by the odd look on Tim's face. When the kid didn't move, he studied him carefully. "And you don't care?"

"Sure we do," Jeremy answered, fingering his badge. "We had to take care of some important business first."

Business? Drew straightened, his senses came alert. He followed the boys' fixed gaze to the holding cell behind him.

Leslie was behind bars!

"What's going on here?" Drew demanded. "Why is your mother locked up in there?"

"We're deputies now," Jeremy answered stoutly. "She's in there because we arrested her."

"Arrested your mother?" Drew turned to gaze at Leslie—the last person he would have expected to find behind bars. "Why? What did she do?"

"All we asked her to do was to ask you to marry her, but she won't listen to us," Jeremy answered. "We figured if she's locked up, maybe she'll have to do it or we won't let her out."

"Sounds to me you've got it backward," Drew replied. "We men usually do the asking. But I guess it makes some kind of weird sense at that." Drew sauntered up to the bars and carefully studied Leslie. "And how do you feel about this marriage stuff?" he asked politely.

"If I hadn't wanted to be here in the first place," she answered, her green eyes flashing, "what makes you think those boys could have gotten me inside the cell? But I'm not going to propose!"

"Guess you're right at that," Drew answered. "It's another one of those men things."

It was then he noticed Leslie had gone home long enough to change into jeans and a T-shirt. As she turned her head, he saw her hair was a silken mass of auburn curls hanging around her shoulders and drawn back with a green ribbon that matched her eyes. Eyes that had softened as she turned back to gaze at him. And lips that begged to be kissed.

Drew was afraid to believe what his eyes were telling him.

He winked at the boys. "I hear Maddie has some

fresh cookies waiting for you across the street,'' he suggested with a get-out-of-here gesture.

The boys tumbled over themselves rushing out the door.

"The kids are partially right," he said as he turned back to Leslie. "Now that I have you where you have to listen, I have a question for you."

"Ask away," she answered. Her expression was enigmatic as she folded her arms across her chest.

"If I told you I've decided to turn in my walking shoes, would you believe me?"

"Depends on what you plan on doing next."

At the longing that came into Drew's eyes, Leslie felt free for the first time in years.

She wanted to laugh at the expression on his face, to shout her sheer joy at the change in him. In both of them.

"Good enough," Drew replied. "I intend to apply for the full-time job of deputy sheriff in Calico. But only if you'll consider marrying me."

"Marry you?" Leslie's heart raced. She clasped her hands to her breast in an instinctive gesture. This was what she'd longed to hear. From Drew and only Drew. It was the culmination of years of dreaming, hoping and having to make the best of reality.

It was a good thing they were separated by a locked door, or she would have thrown herself into his arms and asked him to forgive her for being such a fool. She wanted to tell him she was more than willing to give them a chance. And most of all, to tell him she loved him. But first she had something to clear up.

"Because of the bet?"

"No," he answered. "Because I fell in love with you. And because I've finally found the treasure at the end of the rainbow I've been searching for all these years. That's you." He reached into his pocket for a key as he spoke and unlocked the barred door to the cell.

"I think we're about to drive a lot of people crazy." Tears filled Leslie's eyes as Drew joined her and closed the door behind him. "They'll never know who tamed who."

"Simple," he answered as he reached for her and gathered her in his arms. "The answer is no one won the bet. As for me, I like you just as you are. And I hope you feel the same way about me. So how about it?" he asked. "Was that a yes or..."

"Yes!" She threw her arms around Drew's neck and lifted her lips for his kiss. In a way, he was wrong, but she'd tell him later. They had both won the bet.

When Leslie kissed him with a longing that equaled his, Drew lost himself in the warmth of her embrace and in the desire that overwhelmed him. His last coherent thought was that the antique bridal quilt with its double wedding ring design she'd been working would surely be ready in time for the marriage ceremony.

There was a scuffing sound outside the jail window. The barrel that stood there fell over with a thud.

"Cool! I told you it would work this time, Tim!"

Head Down Under for twelve tales of heated romance in beautiful and untamed Australia!

Here's a sneak preview of the first novel in
THE AUSTRALIANS

Outback Heat by Emma Darcy
available July 1998

'HAVE I DONE something wrong?' Angie persisted, wishing Taylor would emit a sense of camaraderie instead of holding an impenetrable reserve.

'Not at all,' he assured her. 'I would say a lot of things right. You seem to be fitting into our little Outback community very well. I've heard only good things about you.'

'They're nice people,' she said sincerely. Only the Maguire family kept her shut out of their hearts.

'Yes,' he agreed. 'Though I appreciate it's taken considerable effort from you. It is a world away from what you're used to.'

The control Angie had been exerting over her feelings snapped. He wasn't as blatant as his aunt in his prejudice against her but she'd felt it coming through every word he'd spoken and she didn't deserve any of it.

'Don't judge me by your wife!'

His jaw jerked. A flicker of some dark emotion destroyed the steady power of his probing gaze.

'No two people are the same. If you don't know that, you're a man of very limited vision. So I come from the city as your wife did! That doesn't stop me from being an individual in my own right.'

She straightened up, proudly defiant, furiously angry with the situation. 'I'm *me*. Angie Cordell. And it's time you took the blinkers off your eyes, Taylor Maguire.'

Then she whirled away from him, too agitated by the explosive expulsion of her emotion to keep facing him.

The storm outside hadn't yet eased. There was nowhere to go. She stopped at the window, staring blindly at the torrential rain. The thundering on the roof was almost deafening but it wasn't as loud as the silence behind her.

'You want me to go, don't you? You've given me a month's respite and now you want me to leave and channel my energies somewhere else.'

'I didn't say that, Angie.'

'You were working your way around it.' Bitterness at his tactics spewed the suspicion. 'Do you have your first choice of governess waiting in the wings?'

'No. I said I'd give you a chance.'

'Have you?' She swung around to face him. 'Have you really, Taylor?'

He hadn't moved. He didn't move now except to make a gesture of appeasement. 'Angie, I was merely trying to ascertain how you felt.'

'Then let me tell you your cynicism was shining through every word.'

He frowned, shook his head. 'I didn't mean to hurt you.' The blue eyes fastened on hers with devastating sincerity. 'I truly did not come in here to take you down or suggest you leave.'

Her heart jiggled painfully. He might be speaking the truth but the judgements were still there, the judgements that ruled his attitude towards her, that kept her shut out of his life, denied any real sharing with him, denied his confidence and trust. She didn't know why it meant so much to her but it did. It did. And the need to fight for justice from him was as much a raging torrent inside her as the rain outside.

MEN at WORK

All work and no play? Not these men!

April 1998

KNIGHT SPARKS by Mary Lynn Baxter

Sexy lawman Rance Knight made a career of arresting the bad guys. Somehow, though, he thought policewoman Carly Mitchum was framed. Once they'd uncovered the truth, could Rance let Carly go...or would he make a citizen's arrest?

May 1998

HOODWINKED by Diana Palmer

CEO Jake Edwards donned coveralls and went undercover as a mechanic to find the saboteur in his company. Nothing— or no one—would distract him, not even beautiful secretary Maureen Harris. Jake had to catch the thief—*and* the woman who'd stolen his heart!

June 1998

DEFYING GRAVITY by Rachel Lee

Tim O'Shaughnessy and his business partner, Liz Pennington, had always been close—but never *this* close. As the danger of their assignment escalated, so did their passion. When the job was over, could they ever go back to business as usual?

MEN AT WORK™

Available at your favorite retail outlet!

 HARLEQUIN® Ｖ Silhouette®

Take 2 bestselling love stories FREE

Plus get a FREE surprise gift!

Special Limited-Time Offer

Mail to Harlequin Reader Service®

3010 Walden Avenue
P.O. Box 1867
Buffalo, N.Y. 14240-1867

YES! Please send me 2 free Harlequin American Romance® novels and my free surprise gift. Then send me 4 brand-new novels every month, which I will receive months before they appear in bookstores. Bill me at the low price of $3.34 each plus 25¢ delivery and applicable sales tax, if any.* That's the complete price, and a saving of over 10% off the cover prices—quite a bargain! I understand that accepting the books and gift places me under no obligation ever to buy any books. I can always return a shipment and cancel at any time. Even if I never buy another book from Harlequin, the 2 free books and the surprise gift are mine to keep forever.

154 HEN CH7E

Name   (PLEASE PRINT)

Address   Apt. No.

City   State   Zip

This offer is limited to one order per household and not valid to present Harlequin American Romance® subscribers. *Terms and prices are subject to change without notice. Sales tax applicable in N.Y.

UAMER-98   ©1990 Harlequin Enterprises Limited

DEBBIE MACOMBER

invites you to the

HEART OF TEXAS

Join Debbie Macomber as she brings you the lives
and loves of the folks in the ranching community
of Promise, Texas.

If you loved Midnight Sons—don't miss
Heart of Texas! A brand-new six-book series
from Debbie Macomber.

Available in February 1998
at your favorite retail store.

Heart of Texas by Debbie Macomber

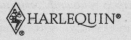

HARLEQUIN®

HPHRT1

Don't miss these Harlequin favorites by some of our bestselling authors!

HT#25721	THE ONLY MAN IN WYOMING	$3.50 U.S.	☐
	by Kristine Rolofson	$3.99 CAN.	☐
HP#11869	WICKED CAPRICE	$3.50 U.S.	☐
	by Anne Mather	$3.99 CAN.	☐
HR#03438	ACCIDENTAL WIFE	$3.25 U.S.	☐
	by Day Leclaire	$3.75 CAN.	☐
HS#70737	STRANGERS WHEN WE MEET	$3.99 U.S.	☐
	by Rebecca Winters	$4.50 CAN.	☐
HI#22405	HERO FOR HIRE	$3.75 U.S.	☐
	by Laura Kenner	$4.25 CAN.	☐
HAR#16673	ONE HOT COWBOY	$3.75 U.S.	☐
	by Cathy Gillen Thacker	$4.25 CAN.	☐
HH#28952	JADE	$4.99 U.S.	☐
	by Ruth Langan	$5.50 CAN.	☐
LL#44005	STUCK WITH YOU	$3.50 U.S.	☐
	by Vicki Lewis Thompson	$3.99 CAN.	☐

(limited quantities available on certain titles)

AMOUNT	$ _____
POSTAGE & HANDLING	$ _____
($1.00 for one book, 50¢ for each additional)	
APPLICABLE TAXES*	$ _____
TOTAL PAYABLE	$ _____
(check or money order—please do not send cash)	

To order, complete this form and send it, along with a check or money order for the total above, payable to Harlequin Books, to: **In the U.S.:** 3010 Walden Avenue, P.O. Box 9047, Buffalo, NY 14269-9047; **In Canada:** P.O. Box 613, Fort Erie, Ontario, L2A 5X3.

Name: _____

Address: _____ City: _____

State/Prov.: _____ Zip/Postal Code: _____

Account Number (if applicable): _____

*New York residents remit applicable sales taxes.
Canadian residents remit applicable GST and provincial taxes.

Look us up on-line at: http://www.romance.net

AMERICAN ♦ ROMANCE®

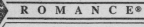

COMING NEXT MONTH

#733 AKA: MARRIAGE by Jule McBride
Big Apple Babies
When Shane Holiday offered marriage to Lillian Smith so she could adopt a baby, he did it to get close to the woman he'd tracked for seven years. But what started as marriage with an agenda suddenly had Shane thinking he was a husband and daddy for real!

#734 THE COWBOY & THE SHOTGUN BRIDE by Jacqueline Diamond
The Brides of Grazer's Corners
One minute Kate Bingham was about to say "I do," the next she was swept off her feet by sexy fugitive Mitch Connery. Although Mitch was innocent, Kate's newly awakened desires were not!

#735 MY DADDY THE DUKE by Judy Christenberry
When her grandmother, the Dowager Duchess, put out an APB on her dad as the World's Most Eligible Bachelor traveling in the U.S. to find a wife, little Penelope Morris went along with her father's disguise as typical Americans. As long as he stayed close to Sydney Thomas, who Pen handpicked to be her new mommy!

#736 DADDY 101 by Jo Leigh
Along with the fortune he had inherited, Alex Bradlee got a set of rules for love. They'd served him well…until he met Dr. Dani Jacobson, who had some rules of her own, the first of which was "Run—don't walk—away." But her daughter had other ideas….

AVAILABLE THIS MONTH:

#729 WANTED: DADDY
Mollie Molay

**#730 THE BRIDE TO BE…
OR NOT TO BE?**
Debbi Rawlins

#731 HUSBAND 101
Jo Leigh

#732 FATHER FIGURE
Leandra Logan

Look us up on-line at: http://www.romance.net